Saving
ZOLA

SLEEPER SEALS, BOOK FOUR

BECCA JAMESON

F₅TOKER 2-12-18

Saving Zola
Copyright © 2017 by Becca Jameson
Print Edition

eBook ISBN: 978-1-946911-15-5
Print ISBN: 978-1-946911-16-2

Cover Artist: Scott Carpenter
Editor: Christa Desir

ACKNOWLEDGEMENTS

I'd like to thank Susan Stoker for allowing me to use one of the characters from her SEAL of Protection series. Tex is a beloved character who just keeps on going!

I'd also like to thank the eleven wonderful ladies who invited me to contribute to this world! You all rock! It was so much fun writing in a multi-author series.

Thanks to my editor, Christa Desir, for her hard work. This one was a royal pain in her butt. Nevertheless, I am still living, and she is still editing for me!

I'd also like to thank my cover artist, Scott Carpenter, for once again creating the perfect sexy cover!

ABOUT THE BOOK

The Sleeper SEALs are former U.S. Navy SEALs recruited by a new CIA counter-terror division to handle solo dark ops missions to combat terrorism on U.S. soil.

Each story in this multi-author branded series is a standalone novel and the series can be read in any order.

Saving Zola is the fourth book in the Sleeper SEALs series. If you are a fan of my Underground series, you'll recognize the hero of *Saving Zola*, Mike Dorsen. He was a member of the FBI team working on the case that spanned several books in The Underground series.

Saving Zola:

They thought they were risking their lives, but they didn't realize the risk was to their hearts.

Zola Carver has worked her entire life to get where she is—assistant district attorney. She doesn't have time for threats from a presumed terrorist group.

Mike Dorsen has made a life for himself, moving from foster care, to a master's in biology, to the SEALs, and finally the FBI. When he gets an assignment from a clandestine faction of the CIA while on vacation, the last person he expects to have in his care is his high school girlfriend, Zola.

Unanswered questions haunt the childhood sweethearts as they reconnect. Their love has never faded, but will secrets held for over a decade tear them apart a second time?

While Zola and Mike run from a terrorist group intent on eliminating Zola, they must find their way back into each other's hearts as easily as they found their way back into bed.

Prologue

ZOLA CLOSED HER eyes, tipped her head back, and moaned. She didn't even care who heard her, though it was unlikely anyone would hear a thing over the din of noise from this crowded party. She gripped the quilt at her sides with both hands in attempt to ground herself any way possible.

"Geez, Zola. You make me so damn horny when you do that," Mike whispered against her bare stomach, his lips teasing her belly button. Inching his way up her body, he continued to nibble a path between her breasts as he shoved her blouse over them.

Zola shuddered as the cooler air in the room hit her skin. She licked her lips, tipped her chin down, and tried to focus on his face when she felt him staring at her.

His expression was intent. "We don't have to do this."

She rolled her eyes. "Stop being so altruistic. I want you to make love to me. I've wanted it for two years."

He fingered the silk material at her neck. "This is a big deal, babe. I don't want you to regret it later."

She released the quilt and grabbed his shirt, dragging it up over his head, forcing him to let her pull it off his arms. "I will never ever regret what we have together. You know that."

She had been trying to convince him to have sex with her for months. Time was running out. They had graduated from high school eight weeks ago. She would be leaving for Yale in a few days. He was going to the University of California, Berkeley.

Just thinking about the distance made her chest tighten.

Lifting up on her elbows to meet his gaze more fully, she threaded her fingers into the back of his longish dark hair and tugged his mouth toward her. "I don't give a shit what anyone else says or thinks, I want this. Don't move to the other side of the country and leave me wondering what it might have felt like. I don't want to give my virginity to someone else. I want it to be *you*."

He stared at her. "Your dad…"

"Is not at this party. Please don't bring him up again."

"He would kill me."

"I'm over eighteen. You're over eighteen. He can't do anything to us."

Mike swallowed, nodding. "Okay." His lips met hers, and the rest of the world ceased to exist.

Zola sighed into his mouth, incredibly grateful one of their mutual friends was having this end-of-summer party and had offered Zola a room for the night. It couldn't have been more perfect.

Mike angled his head to one side and deepened the

kiss, his tongue darting around inside her mouth, dancing with hers, driving her arousal higher. He'd been a fantastic kisser from their first date sophomore year. He'd also been her first boyfriend, so she had no one to compare him to.

After two years of listening to her girlfriends talk about their sexual experiences, she knew what she had with Mike was different. Every time he touched her, she lit up. Her nipples stood at attention. Wetness pooled between her legs.

While the other girls spoke of sloppy kisses and quick fucks in the backs of cars, Zola had felt bad for them. She'd known for over a year that Mike would be a wonderful lover. Unfortunately, he'd always been a bit too respectful of her. He held her hand. He kissed her goodnight. He set a palm on the small of her back.

But he never let things go much further.

The number of times he had groped her could be counted on one hand. And those instances hadn't included more than her breasts. The one time he'd actually opened her blouse and popped her bra, he had stared at her for so long she'd started to shiver. When he finally cupped both globes and then leaned in to reverently kiss her nipples, a piece of her heart had melted.

That had been right after graduation two months ago. He hadn't done it again. In fact, she'd only seen him a handful of times during the summer and always in public.

She could thank her dad for that. Richard Carver did not approve of Mike Dorsen, and he let it be known every time she went out the door. He had gotten her an internship at his law firm over the summer and kept her so damn busy she hardly saw a single friend, let alone Mike.

Her attention jerked back to the present as Mike's hand eased up her side and cupped her lace-covered breast.

She let herself fully relax against the pillow, and he kissed a path toward her ear. "You have no idea what you do to me," he whispered.

She disagreed, but didn't have the ability to argue. Her brain wasn't shooting comprehensible messages to her mouth.

Lowering himself down her body, he slowly slid every button through its hole on her blouse while he nibbled around the edge of her bra. By the time he spread her shirt open, she was shaking with arousal. She gripped his biceps, blinking. "Please…"

"I'm getting there, babe. Don't rush me. I want to remember this for the rest of my life."

She bit her lower lip. She agreed, but her sex was on fire, and her legs were pinned together under him.

He gave a wry grin, as if he knew her plight, and then popped the front clasp of her bra. It fell apart quickly, the globes seemingly so swollen they were busting the lace.

Bracing himself on one elbow, he made leisurely circles around her nipples with the pointer of his other hand. "So damn gorgeous."

"Jesus, Mike. Please…" She squirmed beneath him, unable to get him to budge. He was taking his sweet time, and there was no stopping him.

"Stay still, Zola. You're gonna make me blow in my jeans."

That announcement made her freeze. The last thing she

wanted was for him to come before he was inside her. Was that really a possibility?

She lost all train of thought again when he sucked one nipple gently between his lips and then eased his body to one side of her and set his palm on her inner thigh. "Spread your legs for me, babe."

Her breath came in short pants as she complied, willing him to touch her sex. He never had before. She had gone home from numerous dates as sexually frustrated as anyone could possibly be.

Pushing her skirt up, he tentatively stroked one finger over her silk panties. A moan escaped his lips as he set his forehead against her chest, his breath wafting over her nipple. "You're so wet."

"Mmm," was all she could manage as she spread her legs farther and lifted her butt an inch off the bed, encouraging him to continue.

When he dipped his finger under the edge of her panties to graze her lower lips, she stopped breathing. "Shhh, baby. You're so loud."

Was she making audible noises? She threaded her fingers back into his hair and held him against her chest. "I locked the door. No way anyone's going to walk in on us."

He lifted his face, a half grin making his eyes dance. "I'm not worried about anyone else, babe. I'm just trying to keep from coming in my pants."

"Oh." A flush raced up her cheeks. That again.

He rose next to her, releasing her panties, and unzipped the side of her skirt.

She couldn't focus on anything but his broad, muscled

chest as he removed her skirt and then slid her panties down her legs.

When he was done, he shrugged out of his jeans too, taking his underwear with them. And then he knelt between her legs.

Her gaze honed in on his thick erection bobbing between them. She lifted one hand to stroke a finger up the side.

Mike moaned, his head tipping back as he swayed into her touch. A moment later, he grasped her hand in his and pulled it away. "You can't do that."

She continued to stare, wanting to learn the feel of his velvety skin. Instead, he set her hand on the bed at her side. "Please, babe. Not this time." His voice was deeper, gravelly. Not like she'd ever heard it.

She nodded, still staring.

He traced circles around her nipples with both hands while letting her look her fill. When he lightly pinched the swollen buds, she arched her chest off the bed, her eyes rolling back. Before she knew it, he slid down the mattress and settled between her legs. His face was inches from her sex, and he held her legs wider.

She couldn't move. On the one hand, she was mortified to have him staring at her intimate parts. On the other hand, she wanted him to see her. She wanted him to know what he did to her. How wet she was. How swollen. Needy. Aroused.

He pulled her lips apart and stroked one finger through her wetness, making her grab his shoulders with both hands. Ignoring her, he flicked his finger over the bundle of nerves above her slit.

A shudder racked her body. *Jesus...* What the hell was wrong with the girls she heard talking about sex in the locker room? She felt sorry for all of them. This was an earth-changing experience. Nothing like other girls described.

When Mike slid a finger into her tight channel, she lifted her hips. "Damn, you're sexy." He pumped that finger several times and then pulled it out to circle her clit with her moisture. "Tell me what feels good, babe."

"All of it." She dug her nails into his shoulders and held on. "Everywhere you touch me." In fact, it felt good even when he looked at her.

He played with the nub—testing her reactions? Perhaps. It was hard to believe he hadn't been with other girls, but she knew he hadn't. Even though the two of them hadn't had sex, nor had they spent as much time together as they wanted in the last year, she knew beyond a doubt he was faithful.

He pressed harder.

She drew in a sharp breath. "Yeah... God, Mike. Like that."

He continued to play with her clit, experimenting with every sort of touch imaginable. Suddenly, she dug her heels into the mattress as a knot tightened in her belly. Her vision swam. Her mouth fell open. No sound came out.

He flicked his finger over her clit faster.

She tipped her head back, holding on to his shoulders as if her life depended on it. If he stopped, she would die. Sensation rushed to her sex, pleasure racing through her body as a moment in time stood still. It was fleeting. That edge. The point of no return.

And then she was falling, her sex pulsing around his finger as he continued to stroke her. For long moments, it continued. She didn't know up from down.

When she finally began to float back to earth, she found him smiling at her. "You take my breath away. I will never forget this moment in my life." His words were muted by the ringing in her ears.

She reached for his biceps and tugged. "Please, Mike. Don't make me wait any longer."

He lifted onto his knees again, rolled a condom over his girth, and lined himself up with her sex. His face was strained, teeth gritting, as he let the tip slide into her.

It was tight. No lie. It would hurt for a moment. She knew that. She'd heard from other girls. And she did her own research.

His head dipped toward her chest, so she couldn't see his eyes anymore, but she knew they were closed. He was trying to go slow. For her. Everything he did was for her.

She reached for his waist, lifting her torso toward him. "Mike… Please…"

As if she hadn't spoken, he continued to ease into her. So full. So tight. Nerve endings she didn't know existed came to life. Pleading for more even though the stretch was too much.

"Mike. *Now*," she screamed. She would go insane if he didn't thrust all the way in.

Finally, he did as she requested, pushing the last few inches in to the hilt.

She gasped and held her breath, willing herself not to cry out. She bit her lip to keep from making a single noise while her body learned to accommodate his. It took several long moments.

Mike waited. He didn't budge an inch. Not until she told him to. "Move," she murmured. "Do it again."

Every nerve in her body came alive when he pulled slowly back out and then thrust back in. *Yes. Yes, yes, yes.*

He picked up speed, holding himself aloft over her body, his chest grazing her nipples with every thrust.

Exquisite torture. The best kind.

Her insides tightened again, and she knew she was going to have another orgasm. Was that a thing? Did girls have two in a row? She didn't think so.

But she wasn't other girls, apparently.

She was Mike's. And the moment her sex gripped his erection, squeezing it with her second release, he came with her, a garbled, satisfying sound escaping his lips. He thrust one last time and held himself deep inside her.

She gripped his arms as his body jerked.

When he was spent, he lifted his gaze to meet hers, his eyes glazed, a slow smile spreading. "That was entirely worth the wait."

"Indeed." She smiled back. Too bad they wouldn't be able to have a repeat performance any time in the near future. Not living on opposite sides of the country.

He slid out of her and let his body collapse to one side, one leg nestled between hers, one hand cupping her breast, his chest still heaving, his breathing ragged in her ear. "I'll never forget this."

"Neither will I."

They didn't speak again for a long time, his fingers dancing over her skin until she had goosebumps. He chuckled when she shivered.

She pushed him onto his back and snuggled into his side. He would need to get rid of the condom, but not yet. She wasn't ready to let him go yet. "Please don't disappear on me."

"Never, babe." He gave her shoulders a squeeze. "Never."

She set her chin on his chest and met his gaze. "Why do I have this sinking feeling this is goodbye?"

His gaze was serious. "It's not forever. You'll never get rid of me forever. I'll hunt you down even if your father sends you to a nunnery in Siberia."

She giggled. "I don't think they have nunneries in Siberia." She licked her lips and sobered. "I'm going to miss you."

"I'll miss you too. But it's only four years. We have our entire lives in front of us."

"I don't like it."

"I know, babe, but it makes your father happy for you to go to his alma mater. And besides, you've wanted to be a lawyer for as long as I've known you. I can't let my scholarship to Berkeley go either. So we'll deal."

"Promise?"

"Swear."

Chapter One

Twelve years later…

RETIRED NAVY COMMANDER Greg Lambert leaned forward to rake in the pile of chips his full house had netted him. Tonight he would leave the weekly gathering not only with his pockets full, but his pride intact.

The scowls he earned from his poker buddies at his unusual good luck were an added bonus.

They'd become too accustomed to him coming up on the losing side of five card stud. It was about time he taught them to never underestimate him.

Vice President Warren Angelo downed the rest of his bourbon and stubbed out his Cuban cigar. "Looks like Lady Luck is on your side tonight, Commander."

After he neatly stacked his chips in a row at the rail in front of him, Greg glanced around at his friends. It occurred to him right then, this weekly meeting wasn't so different from the joint sessions they used to have at the Pentagon during his last five years of service.

The location was the secretary of state's basement now,

but the gathering still included top ranking military brass, politicians, and the director of the CIA, who had been staring at him strangely all night long.

"It's about time the bitch smiled my way, don't you think? She usually just cleans out my pockets and gives you my money," Greg replied with a sharp laugh as his eyes roved over the spacious man-cave with envy, before they snagged on the wall clock.

It was well past midnight, their normal break-up time. He needed to get home, but what did he have to go home to? Four walls and Karen's mean-as-hell Chihuahua who hated him. Greg stood, scooted back his chair, and stretched his shoulders. The rest of his poker buddies quickly left, except for Vice President Warren Angelo, Benedict Hughes with the CIA, and their host tonight, Percy Long, the Secretary of State.

Greg took the last swig of his bourbon then set the glass on the table. When he took a step to leave, they moved to block his way to the door. "Something on your minds, gentleman?" he asked, their cold, sober stares making the hair on the back of his neck stand up.

It wasn't a comfortable feeling, but one he was familiar with from his days as a Navy SEAL. That feeling usually didn't portend anything good was about to go down. But neither did the looks on these men's faces.

Warren cleared his throat and leaned against the mahogany bar with its leather trimmings. "There's been a significant amount of chatter lately." He glanced at Ben. "We're concerned."

Greg backed up a few steps, putting some distance

between himself and the men. "Why are you telling me this? I've been out of the loop for a while now." Greg was retired, and bored stiff, but not stiff enough to tackle all that was wrong in the United States at the moment or fight the politics involved in fixing things.

Ben let out a harsh breath then gulped down his glass of water. He set the empty glass down on the bar with a sigh and met Greg's eyes. "We need your help, and we're not going to beat around the bush," he said, making Greg's short hairs stand taller.

Greg put his hands in his pockets, rattling the change in his right pocket and his car keys in the left while he waited for the hammer. Nothing in Washington, D.C. was plain and simple anymore. Not that it ever had been.

"Spit it out, Ben," he said, eyeballing the younger man. "I'm all ears."

"Things have changed in the US. Terrorists are everywhere now," he started, and Greg bit back a laugh at the understatement of the century.

He'd gotten out before the recent INCONUS attacks started, but he was still in service on 9/11 for the ultimate attack. The day that replaced Pearl Harbor as the day that would go down in infamy.

"That's not news, Ben," Greg said, his frustration mounting in his tone. "What does that have to do with me, other than being a concerned citizen?"

"More cells are being identified every day," Ben replied, his five o'clock shadow standing in stark contrast to his now paler face. "The chatter about imminent threats, big jihad events that are in the works, is getting louder."

"You do understand that I'm no longer active service, right?" Greg shrugged. "I don't see how I can be of much help there."

"We want you to head a new division at the CIA," Warren interjected. "Ghost Ops, a sleeper cell of SEALs to help us combat the terrorist sleeper cells in the US…and whatever the hell else might pop up later."

Greg laughed. "And where do you think I'll find these SEALs to sign up? Most are deployed over—"

"We want *retired* SEALs like yourself. We've spent millions training these men, and letting them sit idle stateside while we fight this losing battle alone is just a waste." Ben huffed a breath. "I know they'd respect you when you ask them to join the contract team you'd be heading up. You'd have a much better chance of convincing them to help."

"Most of those guys are like me, worn out to the bone or injured when they finally give up the teams. Otherwise, they'd still be active. SEALs don't just quit." *Unless their wives were taken by cancer and their kids were off at college, leaving them alone in a rambling house when they were supposed to be traveling together and enjoying life.*

"What kind of threats are you talking about?" Greg asked, wondering why he was even entertaining such a stupid idea.

"There are many, more every day. Too many for us to fight alone," Ben started, but Warren held up his palm.

"The president is taking a lot of heat. He has three and a half years left in his term, and taking out these threats was a campaign promise. He wants the cells identified and the

SAVING ZOLA

terror threats eradicated quickly."

These two, and the president, sat behind desks all day. They'd never been in a field op before, so they had no idea the planning and training that took place before a team ever made it to the field. Training a team of broken-down SEALs to work together would take double that time because each knew better than the rest how things should be done, so there was no "quick" about it.

"That's a tall order. I can't possibly get a team of twelve men on the same page in under a year. That's if I can find them." Why in the hell was he getting excited, then? "Most are probably out enjoying life on a beach somewhere." Exactly where he would be with Karen if she hadn't fucking died on him as soon as he retired four years ago.

"We don't want a *team*, Greg," Percy Long corrected, unfolding his arms as he stepped toward him. "This has to be done stealthily because we don't want to panic the public. If word got out about the severity of the threats, people wouldn't leave their homes. The press would pump it up until they created a frenzy. You know how that works."

"So let me get this straight. You want individual SEALs, sleeper guys who agree to be called up for special ops, to perform solo missions?" Greg asked, his eyebrows lifting. "That's not usually how they work."

"Unusual times call for unusual methods, Greg. They have the skills to get it done quickly and quietly," Warren replied, and Greg couldn't argue. That's exactly the way SEALs operated—they did whatever it took to get the job done.

15

Ben approached him, placed his hand on his shoulder, as if this was a tag-team effort, and Greg had no doubt that it was just that. "Every terrorist or wanna-be terror organization has roots here now. Al Qaeda, the Muslim Brotherhood, ISIS, or the Taliban—you name it. They're not here looking for asylum. They're actively recruiting followers and planning events to create a caliphate on our home turf. We can't let that happen, Greg, or the United States will never be the same."

"You'll be a CIA contractor, and can name your price," Warren inserted, and Greg's eyes swung to him. "You'll be on your own in the decision making. We need to have plausible deniability if anything goes wrong."

"Of course," Greg replied, shaking his head. If anything went south, they needed a fall guy, and that would be him in this scenario. Not much different from the dark ops his teams performed under his command when he was active duty.

God, why did this stupid idea suddenly sound so brilliant? Why did he think he might be able to make it work? And why in the hell did he suddenly think it was just what he needed to break out of the funk he'd been living in for four years?

"I can get you a list of potential hires, newly retired SEALs, and the president says *anything* else you need," Warren continued. "All we need is your commitment."

The room went silent, and Greg looked deeply into each man's eyes as he pondered a decision. What the hell did he have to lose? If he didn't agree, he'd just die a slow, agonizing death in his recliner at home. At only forty-seven and still fit, that could be a lot of years spent in that chair.

"Get me the intel, the list, and the contract," he said, and a surge of adrenaline made his knees weak.

He was back in the game.

Chapter Two

MIKE DORSEN PICKED up the phone as he leaned back in his Adirondack chair and stared at the ocean waves wafting toward the shore. The view was so fucking amazing he didn't want to miss a moment of it. The sun was setting, and the wind was picking up, but this was his first vacation in years, and he intended to enjoy every second.

He hadn't recognized the incoming number, but that wasn't unusual. Calls came in to him from all over the place any day of the week. That was the nature of working for the FBI. Even though he was on leave, the calls never stopped.

"Dorsen speaking."

"Is this Mike Dorsen?" The voice wasn't familiar.

Mike stiffened. "It is. Can I help you?"

"Yes. You don't know me, but my name is Greg Lambert. I'm a retired commander from the US Navy."

Mike tilted his head to one side, getting a better grip on his cell. "Okay."

"You're a difficult man to track down."

"Intentionally. I'm on vacation."

"An extended one, I hear."

Mike frowned. How did this man know so much about him? "No rule against that." He'd taken a leave of absence after dealing with a grueling investigation for the FBI in Chicago. He still shuddered every time he thought about all the people who'd lost their lives at the hands of the Russian mafia in the name of science. "How can I help you?"

"I'll cut right to the chase. I got your name from a mutual friend. I need you to do a job for the US government."

"The government? I work for the FBI. Why wouldn't they contact me themselves?" Unease crept up his spine.

"Because this isn't related to the FBI, nor is it above the table. This is a job for someone capable, who isn't afraid to get their hands dirty. I'm looking for a SEAL, Mike."

Mike flinched. He had been a SEAL. He'd worked his ass off to become one only to have the job slip through his hands after four years when his kneecap got shattered in a raid during his second tour to the Middle East. Few people knew he'd been a SEAL, not even inside the FBI. "Who are you working for again?"

"I'm working for the government, the CIA specifically, but the job is under the table. You'll be paid heftily for your service, but no one will ever know you were involved."

"You realize how sketchy that sounds, right? If I had any sense, I'd hang up the phone and block your number."

Lambert chuckled briefly. "Yeah. I get that a lot."

"You've made other similar calls?"

"Several. Yes. Listen, can we meet? I know you're in

Norfolk. I just need an hour of your time. I'm not far from you."

"I suppose you also know where I'm staying?" He rolled his eyes toward the sky, cussing silently inside. Why did he know he was not going to like whatever this Greg Lambert had to say?

"Yes. You free this evening? We could meet someplace neutral, but it would be easier if I came to you so we would have the privacy this conversation deserves."

Mike inhaled slowly. "Fine. Come at seven." He ended the call and leaned back again. "Fuck." Somehow he knew his perfect little getaway was about to go up in smoke.

AS GREG TOOK a seat on Mike's cozy back porch, he rubbed his hands together, staring out at the ocean. "Your view is amazing."

"Yes. It is." Mike was leery. His skin had been crawling from the moment his phone rang that afternoon. Now, he was itching to get this meeting out of the way. "Tell me what you're here for, Lambert."

Greg sighed and leaned back, angling his body to face Mike. "I'm sure it wouldn't shock you to hear there are terrorist sleeper cells all over the country doing their best to undermine us."

Mike glared at him. That didn't require a response.

Greg chuckled. "Okay, well, my job is to put those cells out of commission."

"And you think I can help how?"

"I know your background is in biology. I also know

your last assignment was with the FBI, putting an end to a Russian scheme that involved an experimental drug that would have seriously altered humanity."

Mike winced. Okay, so this guy knew shit. A lot of shit. "That's completely classified."

"Yep." Greg didn't meet his gaze. He continued to stare at the ocean. Cocky. Confident. Knowledgeable.

"And what exactly do you need me for?"

"Got a situation with a senator. Intel suggests a group of terrorists is planning to use biological warfare against him."

Mike held back a gasp. "Right here? On US soil?"

"That's what I'm saying."

A few moments of silence passed. Mike closed his eyes. It wasn't as though he could turn this guy down if it meant the life of a senator. "Look, I know my biological warfare. I've worked in the field. Sure. But you're talking about a serious ballgame. Why me?"

"Because you're available. In the area. And a SEAL." Greg turned to face Mike, leaning his elbows on his knees. "I need someone with stealth."

"And you want me to do what? Play bodyguard to a senator?"

"Nope." Greg shook his head. "His daughter. And while you're at it, perhaps you could catch this motherfucker and kill him for us."

Mike stared at the man, trying to process what he really meant. "His kid? You want me to guard a kid?"

Greg shook his head again. "Not a child. A grown woman. She's a lawyer. Assistant district attorney in New

Haven, Connecticut. She's been getting threatening mail and emails. The threats have gotten closer together and more disturbing. Perhaps she defended the wrong guy or put the wrong guy in jail. Who knows? But our bad guy seems to have chosen to fuck with her to get to her father."

Mike froze, staring at the ocean. "Fuck," he muttered.

Chapter Three

TWO HOURS LATER, Mike sat in the dark living room, nursing a fantastic scotch and staring at the thick file Greg Lambert left him. There was enough light streaming in from the moon to keep him mellow.

He'd agreed to take the job. What choice did he have?

He didn't need to open the file to know exactly who he'd been tasked with protecting. Connecticut had two senators, and only one of them had a daughter who was an assistant district attorney. The second he had his hands on the paperwork, his vacation was history, and his world would forever change course.

"Fuck," he repeated to the room at large for the tenth time. He ran a hand through his hair and took another sip of the scotch. He needed a haircut. It was overdue. Random thoughts to avoid the elephant in the room. As long as he left that folder sitting on the coffee table, its contents remained a secret.

Oh, who was he kidding?

Finally, he gave in. No way would he be able to sleep

anyway with that damn file folder waiting for his attention.

Setting his glass on the end table, he reached for the folder and dragged it onto his lap. With a deep breath, he turned on the light next to him, hating the way it broke through the darkness as if announcing itself as the defining moment when his vacation was officially ruined.

He flipped open the manila folder and picked up the top page.

Senator Richard Carver of Connecticut…

Mike swallowed hard, forcing himself to continue reading and accept this new reality.

Daughter, Zola Carver, Undergraduate—Yale University, pre-law. Law school—Yale University…

It was time to pull his shit together and get his head in the game. Zola was in danger. She needed him. He could no more have turned this job down than he could have cut off his own right arm.

For long moments, he read that first page, learning everything he could about Senator Carver and his daughter before dropping the paper on top of the stack. He leaned his head back and closed his eyes.

Senator Carver had spent years lobbying to make it more difficult for terrorists to infiltrate the US. Among other things, the man obviously spent his life fighting against the ease with which terrorists were able to get into the US, purchase property, travel between states, and even acquire weapons.

Mike shuddered. At least he agreed with the man on his politics concerning this issue. Mike had spent too many nights on two tours of duty fighting the same terrorist organizations that were now infiltrating the US on a daily basis. Whether they came into the country under false pretenses or were homegrown, they still represented the same threat.

According to Greg Lambert, there was an imminent threat against the senator and his daughter. Apparently Zola had participated in several court cases against terrorists.

He hadn't spoken to Zola in twelve years, not since they both left for college. He cringed remembering their final evening together. Best night of his life. Even more than a decade later, he still counted that night as the most important.

After downing the contents of his glass, he reached for the bottle of scotch and poured himself a refill. Leaning back in the armchair, he closed his eyes and let his mind travel down memory lane. He didn't often indulge in prolonged thoughts of Zola, but tonight he felt he had no choice.

He needed to face his past. Tomorrow.

He groaned inwardly as he remembered their final night together. The night he'd lost his virginity. And she hers. The last time he'd spoken to her. The last time he'd communicated with her at all.

He was a dick.

If he had an ounce of common sense, he would call Greg Lambert and tell him there was no way in hell he could take this job. The moment he walked into Zola's life, she was likely to slam the door in his face.

On the flip side, what choice did he have? No way was

he going to turn the job over to someone else. What if that guy couldn't keep her safe? He would never be able to forgive himself if anything happened to Zola.

Nope.

This was on him. He needed to swallow his pride, go to her house, face her head-on, and then, when all the pleasantries were over, he needed to protect her with his own life.

Not one damn thing would happen to Zola Carver on his watch.

Ever.

She might not like it, but the truth was he was good at his job. One of the best. It didn't matter that he'd left the SEALs three years ago. His training was ingrained in him.

It had taken over a year for him to gain full use of his left knee after replacement surgery and therapy, but he'd come back. He was as fit today as he'd been on tour. The new knee wasn't perfect. It sometimes ached. He often worked himself too hard. But when push came to shove, he could ignore the lingering pain and do what needed to be done.

Keeping Zola alive needed to be done.

His adrenaline already pumped through his system. He'd told Lambert he needed a day or two to sort his shit. But no fucking way was he wasting another day with Zola's life on the line. He would arrange to meet with her first thing tomorrow, deal with her wrath, and move on to the part where he kept her ass alive.

No matter what.

AT ELEVEN O'CLOCK the following morning, Mike took a deep breath, wiped his sweaty palms on his jeans, and lifted one hand to knock on the door to Zola's condo.

Luckily, he'd gotten the first flight out of Norfolk that morning and rented a car in Hartford for the drive down to New Haven. Meanwhile, Lambert had informed Zola that her bodyguard was due to arrive before noon.

Apparently, she had rearranged her busy schedule to meet with Mike at her condo.

Mike hadn't said a word to Lambert concerning his previous relationship with the woman he was supposed to protect. He had no way of knowing if Lambert had given his name to Zola or simply told her someone would be arriving to provide protection.

Even though Mike had faced off with more enemies than he could count during two tours, most of whom would have given their own wife and children to ensure Mike was killed, he'd never been as nervous as he was at this moment.

Twelve long years.

A lifetime.

What the hell was he about to face?

He flinched when he heard the handle of the door turning before it opened.

And then the world stopped spinning.

There she was. In the flesh. The girl he'd loved more than himself for more than two years in their teens. The girl he'd pledged to never forget. The girl who'd given him her heart and her virginity.

She blinked, her body stiff, her fingers white where she

held the doorframe too tightly. "Mike?"

She was every bit as gorgeous as she'd been twelve years ago.

No. That was a lie. She was so much prettier now. Wiser. Older. Cultured. An adult. Definitely no longer a girl.

Her strawberry-blond hair might have been a shade darker, but her skin was just as smooth and pale. And her eyes... Shit. That color of green had mesmerized him every time he'd looked at her.

He cleared his throat and licked his lips. "Zola." He couldn't help but let his gaze roam up and down her body. She was even sexier than he remembered too. More filled out. A woman. Her hips were wider. Her breasts fuller. Even her face was softer.

She'd been too skinny when they were younger. She was fucking amazing today.

"What are you doing here?" She glanced past him. "I'm expecting..." Her gaze jerked back to his. She swallowed. "I'm expecting *you*, aren't I?"

"Yes." He continued to stand outside her door, letting her acclimate to the knowledge that he was back in her life, information he'd had for thirteen hours. Information she had a right to process. Obviously she hadn't been expecting him.

He forced deep breaths, his hands hanging loosely at his sides. He didn't want to cross his arms and create a subconscious barrier between them.

Seconds ticked by. She blinked, staring at him. Her gaze also wandered up and down his body. "You look good," she whispered, though he wasn't sure she intended to say that out loud.

"You do too, Zola. May I come in?" he prompted.

"Right. Of course." She stepped back, releasing the doorframe and opening the door wider.

He stepped past her, entering her home for the first time. The deep breath he took for fortification was a mistake. Every memory crashed back around him as her scent reached deep into his soul.

Zola stepped around him, notably not touching him.

Could he blame her?

"Come in." She headed deeper into her space, leaving him to watch her from behind.

For a moment, he simply stood frozen, staring at her fantastic ass encased in a pencil skirt. The spike heels she wore made her legs even longer than he remembered.

At eighteen, she had already carried herself with an air of importance, having been bred to keep her shoulders back and her head high. At thirty, she had clearly perfected the art.

He reminded himself she was a lawyer. And not just any lawyer. She was already an assistant district attorney in the New Haven office. Did her job play a role in the threats to her life? Lambert and the file had suggested as much.

As he glanced around her condo, he wondered how she could afford such a nice place. No doubt she barely made a passing wage from the district attorney's office. And this condo was worth more than she could afford. Of course, her father was a state senator who came from money.

Zola headed straight for the kitchen that was attached

to the living room, separated only by a dining area. The layout was modern and the design was sleek. It had been remodeled at some point, undoubtedly knocking out walls to open up the space.

She rounded the breakfast bar, still not speaking, and grabbed the coffee pot, filling two mugs before lifting her gaze. "Do you still take it black?"

"Yes." He nearly choked on the word. She remembered how he took his coffee?

After she slid one mug across the counter to where he stood on the other side, she lifted her own with both hands and took a sip. Did she need the caffeine to give her strength? Or was she hiding behind the mug as a defensive strategy?

"You're working for the district attorney," he commented to break the ice.

"Yes. It's not a glamourous job, but it's where my heart lies. Of course, the CIA seems to think one or more of the people I've helped convict may be directly or indirectly attempting to kidnap me. I'll tell you right now, I don't buy it."

He lifted a brow. "Seriously?"

She nodded. "Lawyers get threats all the time. It's part of the job. Mine is no different from anyone else's."

Ah, so she wanted to cut right to the chase. "I'm under the impression the threats coming to you have more to do with your father's position as senator than your own work."

"Yes. That's what they tell me." She rolled her eyes. "My father has been working hard on legislature that would help us indict more suspected terrorists in civilian court.

Nevertheless, it's a stretch."

Mike took a sip of the steaming coffee and set the mug on the counter. "With all due respect, Zola, a clandestine section of the CIA hired me under the table to protect your life. I'm inclined to take that very seriously. Would it be possible for us to operate under the assumption that the government doesn't throw money away for no good reason and assume they must have sufficient evidence to support my standing in your kitchen today?" He forced himself to keep his voice level. It was an art. Though it was admittedly difficult while facing his childhood sweetheart—a woman with a possible death wish.

Zola stared at him for long moments, her expression giving nothing away. Finally, she sighed, at the same time allowing her shoulders to sag. "Let's say, for the sake of argument, that someone would like to kidnap or even kill me, are you planning to follow me around indefinitely until this terrorist is apprehended?" She visibly shuddered as though the thought of spending even two minutes in Mike's company gave her goosebumps.

Mike set his hands on her counter and leaned forward, waiting until he had her full attention—her gaze fixed on his—before he spoke again. He was a little put off by her flippant attitude. "Actually, Zola, my plan would be to kill the motherfucker who dares to threaten you with my bare hands sooner rather than later."

Zola gasped, her mouth falling open.

He didn't intend to get defensive, but his next words couldn't be interpreted any other way. "So, yes. I do indeed intend to latch on to your side for the foreseeable future until the threat is dispelled. But, as it turns out, I'm pretty good at my job. So you won't have to worry about my disruption in your life for any longer than absolutely necessary."

Her lips slowly closed, and she licked across the bottom one and then the top one.

It was all he could do to keep from moaning at the fullness of those rosy lips. Lips he remembered tasting more times than he could count as if the last such occurrence had been yesterday.

"I'm in the middle of a case," she pointed out, her voice holding far less conviction than a minute ago.

"And I'm under the impression your boss, the district attorney, has been informed of your situation and is prepared to deal with your temporary absence from the office with the understanding you will continue to work remotely and check in twice daily. I got us a burner phone, and you can use my secure computer. You'll need to leave yours behind in case they're bugged."

Mike had done his homework. He'd studied her file cover to cover. He'd spoken with Lambert early that morning and then again on his way to her condo.

Zola closed her eyes as she took another sip of her coffee. Finally, she set it down, seemingly resigned. "Fine. What's the plan?"

Without flinching, he spoke. "I have a vacation home I've been renting for the month. We could return there if you'd like, or if you have another destination in mind, I'll let go of my rental and we can make other plans."

"Where?"

"Norfolk."

"Virginia?"

"Is there another?" he teased, forcing a small smile.

She narrowed her gaze. "It's just that it's February. And it's cold. You chose a beach property in the Northeast? Why not Florida or San Diego?"

Mike shrugged. "I don't mind the cold. And I'm not the sort of person who needs to surf or lie in the sun. I just wanted peace and quiet for a month or two before taking my next assignment."

"How long did that last?"

"Four days."

She winced. "Shit. Bummer."

"Is it?" He lifted a brow. The way he saw it currently, there was every possibility this working vacation wouldn't suck at all. He was going to spend countless days with a woman he once loved more than himself. Unless she had undergone a drastic personality change, he intended to enjoy every moment of her company.

A slow smile spread across Zola's face. "Jury's still out on that one."

Chapter Four

HOLY MOTHER OF God.

What had Zola done in a previous life to deserve this level of insanity?

First, the CIA sends some guy she's never heard of to her doorstep to inform her that her life was in danger and she needed protection, and then two days later, Mike Dorsen steps right out of her past to fill the position.

She had to be dreaming.

And the damn man had to show up looking like a million bucks. He was nothing like the eighteen-year-old boy who took her virginity and then walked away with a smile and a promise.

No. He was a much better, improved version of that teenager. With muscles on every inch of his body, a wry grin that hadn't changed in twelve years, and the beginning of the tiniest of wrinkles around his eyes, he was sex personified.

Just what she did *not* need.

Why couldn't he have been ugly? Balding. Scarred.

Graying. Something. Anything.

She sighed as she changed into slacks and then began stuffing clothes into a suitcase with shaking hands. Who was she kidding? The man would look hotter than sin no matter what the circumstances. His sexiness came from within. One look into his eyes—the gateway to his soul—and any woman would swoon. Nothing physical about him would make a bit of difference.

But it didn't help that he had no flaws.

She was so preoccupied thinking about Mike that she didn't notice him approaching and nearly jumped out of her skin when she turned around to find him leaning against the doorframe. "Jesus. Shit. Mike." She set a hand over her heart as she tried to catch her breath.

"Sorry. I didn't realize you hadn't heard me. I thought you were simply ignoring me."

"Why would I do that?"

He lifted a brow, straightening his frame. "I don't know. Probably because you're pissed."

"Why would I be pissed?"

"Because you're not fond of the idea of running from a possible kidnapper. Because you don't like having your life disrupted. Because the man who showed up at your doorstep was me." His voice dipped lower as he finished.

She flinched. He wasn't wrong.

He continued, his voice even lower, softer. "Because we have a history that leaves you with more questions than answers."

Nail meet head.

She pursed her lips as she turned around to zip her

suitcase. She wasn't sure what all she'd tossed inside haphazardly. Nothing about her behavior was rational or normal. Usually, she was incredibly organized and tidy. Today she felt completely off balance. It had started earlier in the morning when she'd been told she needed to leave work to go meet her mysterious protector. And it had gone downhill from there.

"Zola…" His voice was still soft, but gentler.

She spun around to face him. "Not now. Let's get out of here. You open that Pandora's box and we'll never make it to the airport."

He nodded and came toward her.

For a moment, she worried he would reach out for her. If he touched her, she would fall into a million pieces. But that wasn't his intention. Instead, he hefted her suitcase off the bed and turned around to carry it out of the room.

Zola couldn't decide if she was disappointed he hadn't touched her or relieved. A little of both.

She followed him to the front room, turning off lights and going through a mental checklist of all the things she needed to do before leaving indefinitely. She didn't have pets or even plants. Was that depressing?

The reality was that Zola had worked her ass off for years, first in undergrad, then moving to law school, and then making her way to the DA's office. Every step of the way she met another life goal. Every professional aspiration had been fulfilled.

She didn't care that her only friends were work colleagues and she'd never been in a serious relationship. She didn't have time for that sort of thing. She worked hard to make the world a safer place. It was in her blood.

As she met Mike at the door, she glanced back at the living room. What did she have to show for all her hard work? A clean condo? A tidy appointment book?

Certainly not a man.

They drove to the airport in silence, Zola looking out the window the entire time. Her mind raced. If she didn't keep the memories from twelve years ago at bay, she would lose it. So many snapshots running through her brain.

Her first kiss was with this man.

The first time she lied to her father.

The first time she snuck out of the house.

The first time she snuck him *into* the house.

The first time she had sex…

Every picture in her mind was vivid, as though it had all happened last week instead of more than a decade ago.

What happened to them?

She was afraid of the answer, so she sat next to him with her lips pursed together and her gaze out the window, seeing nothing.

Some supreme being had to have been laughing heartily at this predicament. What were the chances? Of all the people in the world, how had Mike Dorsen been sent to be her bodyguard?

Was this some sort of divine intervention? Or the most twisted joke the universe could conspire against her?

When they got to the airport, she had her first contact with Mike. He set his hand on her back as they moved through the concourse, aiming for the ticket counter. He didn't touch her skin, but the pressure of his fingers against the small of her back sent a shudder up her spine.

She remembered that touch. It nearly burned, and not in a bad way. The heat coming from the tips of Mike's fingers melted a bit of her resolve.

No matter how many times she told herself this was a business arrangement and to leave it at that, she needed answers. For now, she could ignore the questions running through her mind nonstop. Eventually, when they reached their destination, she would have to ask.

What happened?

Why did you leave me?

Mike spoke to the man behind the counter, handed him their driver's licenses, and took the tickets from him. He never once stopped glancing around, always aware of their surroundings as though whoever was interested in Zola was right on their heels. Was he being overly cautious? Or did he know things he hadn't told her?

It wasn't until they were through security, at the gate, and then on the plane that Zola found out they were sitting in first class.

Who paid for this? Surely not the government.

Mike's brow was furrowed as he lifted her suitcase into the overhead bin. He ushered her into the window seat, and then collapsed into the one next to her, running a hand over his face.

"You didn't buy these first class tickets." She didn't ask. It wasn't a question.

"Nope." He didn't meet her gaze. Instead, he leaned his head back, his eyes closed.

Suddenly, she knew who had a hand in this and sighed.

Her father. Of course. And that pissed Mike off?

"I'm sorry," she found herself uttering, wishing immediately she hadn't spoken.

"For what?" He twisted to face her, his eyes drawn close.

"For my father." When they were sixteen, that had been her most-used phrase. When they were seventeen, it continued, increasing in frequency. When they were eighteen, it became a mantra.

She winced, remembering all the times she'd apologized for her father's actions.

Mike frowned, but only for a second. His face suddenly lifted, his eyes widening, his lips switching to a grin. "Did you feel the need to say that out of old habit?"

She smiled back at him. "It just slipped out. But judging from the frustration evident on your face, I'd say my dad paid for this upgrade. You never did like him interfering."

"Nope." He looked away, the lighthearted banter gone. As if he had a sudden need to read the emergency exit plans, he grabbed the trifold piece of card stock from the back of the seat and flipped it around in his hands.

Zola reached across the wide armrest and grabbed his forearm. "He still meddles in my life. Some things never change. But he means well. I'm sure he wanted me to be comfortable. So he upgraded us."

Mike gave his head a quick shake, not meeting her gaze. "Right."

Oh yeah, he was pissed. Some things never changed. Although she wasn't sure this aggravation was warranted.

There was no reason for Mike to go all cold on her just because her dad was kind enough to increase their comfort for the short flight to Norfolk. He didn't have to be a jackass. After all, he was the one who walked away from her and never looked back. He was the one who broke his promises. If anyone should be pissed, it should be her.

"Put your seat belt on, babe. We're gonna take off soon." He changed the subject, still not making eye contact. But the way he said "babe" sent a jolt of electricity through her that was far more intense than when he'd set his hand on her back.

He'd called her *babe* hundreds of times in their youth. Perhaps thousands. In another world. In another lifetime. It dragged forth memories that were better left in the past.

Her hands were shaking as she buckled her seat belt, and she chewed on her lower lip and stared out the window as the plane backed away from the Jetway. Her eyes watered, and she willed them not to leak and embarrass her. There was no logical reason why she should be all choked up over a simple endearment after twelve years of separation. Irrational.

Mike set a hand on her shoulder. "You okay?"

She nodded, fighting harder, not facing him.

Stop being nice.

As the plane made its way to the runway and then sped off, she leaned back in her chair, closed her eyes, and focused on breathing. She could do this. She had no choice.

It was evening before Mike pulled the black Tahoe he'd

rented up to the lake house and shut off the engine. "I'm sorry you won't be able to see much tonight with the sun down. You'll be shocked when you take in the view tomorrow morning. It's amazing."

She didn't respond. They'd spoken so little to each other all day it wasn't surprising. Instead, she meandered along behind him as he grabbed her suitcase from the trunk and then led her to the front door. "It's the backyard you have to see. It exits out to a fantastic patio with the beach for a backdrop." He was rambling, though he had no idea why he felt the need suddenly to break the ice between them.

They were stuck together for the foreseeable future, and though he had no intention of discussing the past with her or dragging up bad feelings, he needed to pull his shit together and make the most of the present.

It would help if she wasn't so damn sexy. She had changed into more practical traveling clothes at her condo, but the fitted black pants she now wore only brought more attention to her perfect ass, not less. The skirt had given him a view of her legs, but the pants... Damn, her ass was fine.

He hoped to God the woman owned jeans, and that they were in the suitcase, because the only thing he could think of that would make his cock harder would be denim stretched across her cheeks.

Mike fumbled with the keys to the house as he shook thoughts of Zola's butt from his mind. Moments later, he had the door open and was dropping her suitcase inside so he could turn to the panel and shut off the alarm.

"Wow, high tech," she said. "They need an alarm on a rental property?"

He nodded. "It's not a random rental. It belongs to a friend of mine. He moved several months ago to live with his fiancée and graciously let me stay here for an extended vacation. I'm paying him peanuts. He wouldn't accept more."

She wandered farther into the space as he flipped on low lighting. "I can see the appeal. It's so cozy."

"Go on out to the patio. Even in the evening, you can see the waves and listen to them crashing against the shore. It's soothing. I think the moon is strong enough to give you a view."

She dropped her purse on the large, brown, soft leather couch quickly, her feet making a beeline for the sliding glass doors off the breakfast area.

Moments later, she was outside, leaving Mike to continue gathering brain cells in her wake. He needed to snap out of it. His job was to protect her, and he couldn't do that from inside while she kicked off her shoes and wandered down the steps and into the sand.

He raced to catch up, knowing how mesmerizing the ocean was and understanding perfectly well why she would head directly for it as if drawn by a magnet. He'd done the same thing four days ago.

Rushing, he kicked off his own shoes, tugged off his socks, and jogged down the steps to catch up with her.

She didn't stop until her feet were buried in the wet sand at the edge of the waves. And then she tipped her head back and closed her eyes. After several deep breaths, she spoke. "God, I miss this. I don't live that far from the ocean. It's ridiculous that I don't make it to the beach more often. It's so relaxing."

She didn't glance his direction, but she had sensed he was nearby. She'd always been sensitive like that. Which would help keep her alive when push came to shove.

"Are you hungry?" he asked to make conversation. They'd eaten in the airport.

"No. I'm good." She lowered her gaze slowly but not to meet his. Instead, she stared at the crashing waves. Suddenly she turned around, marching back to the house. "I think I'll go to bed. I'm exhausted. And I need to read a deposition before I fall asleep."

She was going to read something that boring in bed? He followed her back to the house, grabbed her suitcase, and led her down the short hallway, pointing to the right. "You can take this bedroom. I'm right down the hall." He nodded that direction next. "Bathroom's there." He indicated the guest bath with a flick of his wrist as he set her suitcase inside the bedroom.

"Thanks. I'll see you in the morning." She still didn't look at him as she slid into the room and shut the door softly behind her.

Mike's heart pounded in his chest from her proximity and the knowledge she was still feet away from him. His first love—the only woman he'd ever truly loved—was in this perfect vacation home with him, nothing but a door separating them.

A door and a world of hurt.

His brain told him to keep their relationship strictly

business. Protect her at all costs and go his own way afterward. His heart told him to grab her shoulders, force her to meet his gaze, and delve into the depths of her eyes to see if there was a glimmer of the love they'd felt for each other still simmering.

Shaking himself out of his stupor, he turned toward the kitchen to lock the doors and set the alarm. It wasn't late. It was only seven. He sat at the kitchen table, powered up his computer, and entered the private message room where he knew he could have a secure conversation with the man who owned this house.

John "Tex" Keegan wasn't simply some old friend. He was also a retired SEAL. He'd been wounded in battle himself and then spent years in this amazing beach house working behind the scenes for the military, the FBI, and the CIA. Anyone who needed computer assistance knew who to call.

It wasn't until he met and rescued a woman who became his fiancée that he'd ventured out of his self-imposed shell. And now, he was a new man.

Mike had spoken to Tex many times over the years. The guy was a computer genius. If it needed to be hacked, he could do it. Though the two of them had never officially met, they had a common bond in their SEAL background and their desire to save the world from itself.

When Mike had sent Tex a message last night, letting him know how totally fucked his vacation was, they'd ended up on a secure line discussing the possibilities.

Although Mike would never be able to reveal his contact to anyone, he gave Tex enough information for it to be obvious Mike was taking a job for a secret CIA operation. Tex wouldn't ask questions about who his contact was, but he was embedded deep enough in government issues that he understood the gravity of the situation. Time to fill him in on the last twelve hours.

Mike: *Tex, you there?*

Tex: *Yep. Did you make it back to the house okay?*

Mike: *Yeah.*

Tex: *I can practically hear your sigh through the message board. Lol*

Mike: *You aren't wrong. This is going to be the hardest assignment of my life. Maybe I shouldn't have taken the job. Someone else could have done it. She never would have known the difference.*

Tex: *That bad? Did she read you the riot act?*

Mike: *No. Worse. She hasn't mentioned a thing. It's like we're strangers.*

Tex: *Ouch. Hang in there. She's shocked. You've known she was the person you were sent to protect since last night. I assume she was blindsided upon your arrival?*

Mike: *Definitely.*

Tex: *Listen, I did some digging. Whoever is after your woman is smart. He's hard to nail down. He cleans up his trails.*

Mike flinched as he read the words *your woman*. As if Zola were his. That would never happen.

Mike: *Appreciate the effort. It's above and beyond, man.*

Tex wasn't even getting paid. The man seemed to get off on solving crimes from his laptop though. He'd never turned Mike down for anything.

Tex: *Well, if you get any more information, shoot it my way. In the meantime, I'll see if I can crack this open.*

Mike: *Thanks. Later.*

Tex: *Later.*

Great. A dead end didn't give Mike any sense that this job would be quick. The longer he spent with Zola, the harder it would be to keep himself from falling for her all over again.

Chapter Five

Z OLA WOKE TO the scent of coffee. She moaned as she rolled onto her back and stared at the ceiling. The sun was up high enough that she knew she'd slept late. A squinted glance at the partially closed blinds told her it was about nine.

She'd spent hours the night before forcing herself to memorize every detail in the case folder she'd brought with her. It was meant to take her mind off the sexy SEAL in the other room and prepare her for trial. She wasn't sure either happened. But at least she'd worn herself out and then crashed into bed and slept hard.

With a fortifying breath, she hauled herself out of bed and padded across the room. She'd worn a tank top to bed with nothing else except her panties. After shrugging into a pair of yoga pants and a large sweatshirt from her college days, she stepped into the hallway.

Coffee first.

When she rounded the corner, she stopped in her tracks.

Mike.

Damn him. Why did he have to look so hot? He didn't know she was behind him yet. He stood at the counter in the kitchen doing something in the sink. Sun shined through the window over the sink to cast a warm glow of light around him.

But those details weren't what had her frozen in her spot.

Nope. He was wearing nothing more than low-hanging jeans. She couldn't see his feet, but she would guess they were bare. But his back…

Damn. He was much larger than he'd been in high school, which would stand to reason since he'd been in the navy. But he wasn't an active SEAL now, and he obviously still worked out. It seemed like the muscles in his shoulders and arms and back had muscles of their own.

Suddenly he turned around to set something on the counter behind him. He caught her standing there, and a smile spread across his face. "You're up."

Her mouth was dry. How long had she been staring? She cleared her throat. "Yes. The smell of coffee lured me."

He lifted the pot to indicate it was full and poured her a mug. "Half a scoop of sugar. Splash of cream?"

She nodded as she stepped forward. "How did you know? I didn't drink coffee in high school." She had known his preferences from that stage of life, but he wouldn't know hers.

"You had three cups of coffee yesterday." He half grinned as he stirred.

"Ah." *Right.* She took the mug from him, her breath

catching when their fingers touched. To hide her face and avoid his gaze, she leaned toward the mug and took a sip.

"How late did you stay up?"

"I don't know. Late." She didn't want him to know how hard she'd worked to keep from thinking about him nor how long she'd tossed and turned after finally turning out the lights.

He chuckled. "Well, while you slept the day away, I've been working this morning." He pointed at the kitchen table. His computer sat open, the screen bright. He turned to head that direction, resumed his seat, and nodded toward the chair opposite his.

Yeah…his feet were bare. Sexy as hell. So were hers, but who knew how he felt about feet? She almost laughed at her insane thoughts as she lowered herself onto the seat.

She cleared her throat again, looked out the window to avoid his chest, and spoke. "Why did you leave the SEALs?" Seemed like a good place to start. All she knew was that he had been a SEAL at some point.

"I was injured three years ago in the Middle East." He tapped his leg. "Shot in the knee. Shattered my kneecap."

She winced. She hadn't noticed him limping. "No one would be able to tell now."

He smiled at her again. If he kept doing that, she wouldn't be able to think. "Trust me. If you saw the scars."

She shivered. The idea of seeing his knee… Which would include him not having on his jeans…

He laughed. "Some things about you have not changed."

Her face heated. She knew it would be a deep red as

was always the case when she felt self-conscious. Her pale complexion dictated that every flush was visible to the world.

Mike set his elbow on the table and put his chin on his palm, leaning closer to her. "Sorry. I couldn't help teasing you. How are you still so easily embarrassed at the age of thirty?"

She tucked her lips between her teeth. Not that he required an answer, but if he knew how little experience she had with men, his eyes would bug out.

He kept talking. "Besides, I didn't even say anything except that I have wicked scarring on my knee. How did you twist that into something sexual?"

She still didn't respond, but she did turn a deeper red. Finally, she couldn't remain in his presence, so she pushed back from the table, grabbed her coffee, and headed from the room. "I'm gonna take a shower."

MIKE WATCHED HER walk away, his smile falling as he sobered. Her ass in those tight yoga pants. Lord help him. First the skirt and then the pants and now this. It kept getting worse.

He leaned back in his chair and lifted his hands to fold them behind his head. How was he supposed to keep up this charade with the sexiest woman he ever knew?

When they were young, her rosy cheeks always gave away her shock at the way he spoke to her sometimes. Even though they had only slept together one time, he had teased her mercilessly by whispering things in her ear in public.

Nothing compared to the kinds of things he wanted to say to her now, but at seventeen, even the suggestion of kissing her in front of people made her blush.

She had been a bit of a prude when they first hooked up. In fact, his friends had teased him about dating the school bookworm. But he'd known from the first moment she sat next to him in tenth-grade English that she was someone special.

He didn't care what harassment the other guys dished out. He wanted her bad enough to take it. And he'd never given up. It took a while to convince her to go out with him, and then she'd relented and met him at the movies with a group of people.

She'd been sweet and shy and funny and damn smart and cute as hell. His best friend thought Mike would get over her. After all, she was from the other side of the tracks. Her dad was rich. A politician. She came from money.

Mike was in foster care. The only reason he'd gotten into the small private school they attended was because he'd worked his ass off and had an affinity for science and math.

He'd been lucky. His foster parents had noticed he was bright as soon as he came to live with them in the fourth grade—his third family. They were kind and nurturing, and they met with his teacher and arranged for him to apply to the elite academy where he attended high school.

He knew he was lucky. Foster kids didn't normally do that well in the system. It was rare. And he didn't squander the opportunity. He didn't want to spend his life in poverty on the streets or worse. He didn't want to end up dead from being in the wrong place at the wrong time, caught in the crossfire between gangs.

That had been his father's fate, though Mike didn't remember him. He'd been a baby.

His mother hadn't fared any better. She'd died of an overdose when Mike was four. His memory of her was spotty—a small, skinny woman with stringy hair and gaunt features from years of abuse.

Foster home number one had lasted two years, and he'd hardly spoken to anyone in that house.

Foster home number two had lasted three years, during which time he'd forced himself to join life and started to come out of his shell. He'd realized early on that if he was going to get out of the cycle of poverty and drugs, he had to do it himself.

That family had done the best they could for him, but eventually the father had gotten a job in New York, and he didn't think it was reasonable to take Mike with them. The pain of that separation had been intense. Mike was nine years old and felt so unwanted he could hardly lift his gaze.

And then the Andersons came on the scene. He owed them his life.

Shaking the sad memories from his mind, he focused on the water running in the shower. He closed his eyes, visualizing Zola in that shower, naked, wet. He could tell even without seeing her naked that she had filled out significantly since high school.

He swallowed over the lump in his throat and lowered his arms to adjust his stiffening cock trapped under the zipper of his jeans. Any added weight to the tits he remembered would make them glorious. They'd been fantastic to behold at eighteen. Now… Shit.

The water shut off, and Mike jumped up to take his mug to the sink. He rushed down the hallway to his own room and shut the door to hurry toward the shower himself. He didn't think he could face her again just yet. He needed some time alone.

He needed a plan. What the hell was happening between them? She was a job. Nothing else. He needed to protect her life. Toying with her emotions or getting involved with her wasn't an option.

Was it?

He hoped he could take the edge off his lust in the shower, and it didn't help any when his mind wandered to images of her doing the same thing. Would she? The girl he'd known twelve years ago would never have masturbated in the shower. He smiled again at the image. Contrary to his own little pep talk, he'd give anything to see that show.

Thirty minutes later, he found her sitting at the kitchen table opposite where he was set up, her face tipped down, studying a thick file in front of her. The empty wrapper from a granola bar sat on the table next to her. Good. She'd found something to eat.

As he slid into his seat across from her, she lifted her gaze. "You really think this is all necessary?"

"All what?"

"Me. Hiding here in Norfolk. Over some random threats that probably won't amount to anything."

"You tired of me already?" he teased.

She rolled her eyes. "Can you be serious for a minute?"

"Come here." He motioned with one hand for her to

round the table.

She pushed her chair out and came to his side as he moved his mouse around and opened a file. When she finally stood close enough for him to touch but keeping an obviously intentional distance, he reached for the chair around the side of the table and scooted it next to his. "Sit."

"Bossy," she muttered as she lowered herself onto the seat, dragging it back a few inches.

He smirked. "And stop trying to avoid me. I don't bite. Touching me won't kill you. It's insulting. Have I ever laid a hand on you in anger?"

She gasped.

Good. He needed to make that point. Her avoidance was growing old fast. She'd flinched like he'd burnt her when he handed her a mug of coffee earlier. And yesterday in the airport and on the plane, she had shrunk away from him several times. She acted like he might hit her.

"Of course not. I wasn't thinking that," she muttered.

He turned his torso to face her more fully. "Has someone else hit you? Another man?" That idea hadn't occurred to him before. It was possible, but if it was true, he would kill the guy with his bare hands.

She scrunched up her face. "Do I seem like the kind of woman who would stay in a relationship with an abuser?"

"No. Not at all. But some asshole could have hurt you once before you were aware of his nature and left."

She shook her head. "No. Never. Don't be silly."

"Then you won't mind me touching you." He reached out and grabbed her hand, wrapping his fingers around it from the back.

She jerked her arm back, dislodging him with another more audible gasp.

This wasn't what he was meant to be doing right now. He should be enlightening her on the level of danger she was in because obviously she wasn't as informed as he was. But as soon as she came to his side of the table with her weird need to keep space between them, he'd lost his cool on that topic.

He wasn't a leper. And he'd never given her any reason to cringe away from him—not then, and not now. "What the hell, Zola?"

She lowered her face, tucking her hands between her legs.

He let his gaze follow her hands to the spot where she crushed her fingers between thighs that were now covered with the last material he wanted to see her in—denim. "Talk to me." He softened his voice. "We have to work together. We're stuck together like glue for the foreseeable future. I need to know what I'm dealing with."

"Well, it's not abuse. So let that go."

"Okaaay. No one has mistreated you. Then what?"

When she jerked her face up to meet his gaze, her expression was pained. "Just don't…"

"Don't what, babe?" Now his chest hurt.

"Don't…touch me."

The pain grew more intense. Don't touch her? "Zola, I don't understand."

"It's too much, okay?" Her voice rose. She shoved the chair back and stood. "It brings back memories. And what makes it worse is that you obviously don't feel the same thing. So just stop. When your skin touches mine, my heart races, and I can't think of anything except the last time we were together."

Holy fuck. He couldn't breathe, let alone speak.

She turned around and fled the two feet to the sliding glass doors, and then she raced outside and ran down the steps to the beach.

Mike stared after her for several seconds before shaking his ass in gear and following. She still didn't understand the seriousness of her situation. And if he didn't get control of his lust, he wouldn't be able to protect her.

She headed straight for the edge of the water to stand in the same spot she'd occupied last night. It was chilly outside this morning, and she wrapped her arms around her middle to ward off the wind.

Her gorgeous strawberry-blond hair blew around her back and neck, making him long to thread his fingers in it and tug her head back the way he used to do in high school.

When he reached her, he set his hands tentatively on her shoulders and then smoothed them down her biceps until he wrapped his arms around her body and pulled her back against his chest. He set his chin on the top of her head, relieved that she didn't jerk away from him.

For long minutes, he stared out at the waves with her while she slowly relaxed in his embrace, and then he eased his mouth down to her ear. He used to set his lips on that sensitive spot every day multiple times. It felt like home. "I'm sorry. I should've read you better. I thought…"

What did he think? He assumed she'd moved on. He

assumed she probably had a boyfriend. Why on earth wasn't she married? So sexy. So full of life.

When she didn't respond, he continued, "I didn't think you would still have feelings for me." *Not like the ones I have for you.* He'd never forgotten her. Not for a day. Not in all these years. She had been it for him. He'd known it then, and he still knew it now.

What if she felt the same way? But that was crazy. He knew she had moved on. Found another man. Made a life for herself. After months of wallowing in self-pity over her when he should have been enjoying his freshman year at Berkeley, he'd finally forced himself to let her go.

But this? What was this?

"Why wouldn't I? Seeing you drags it all back." She kept her gaze to the water as she nearly whispered, "Touching you…" She sighed. "It sets my blood on fire, Mike."

He was shocked by her bluntness. And half of him was elated to hear he affected her as much as she did him. Now what should he do? That information was heady.

She squirmed in his embrace. "Let me go. Please."

He held her tighter. "No. I like holding you. And we need to discuss this."

Her chest heaved against his forearms as she stopped struggling. "Can we discuss it without you touching me?"

"No." Suddenly it seemed important that he keep his arms around her. Obviously she had an issue, and he intended to put it to rest. He closed his eyes and breathed in her scent, setting his nose against the skin behind her ear.

She shuddered. "Mike…"

"Babe. It's the same for me. When you touch me, it's like an electric current runs between us. So we need to work it out."

"We can do that without you holding me." Her voice held no conviction.

"We can do it *with* me holding you." He squeezed tighter.

She set her hands on his forearms and returned the firm grip. Blessed angels.

He wasn't sure where to begin. And it turned out he didn't have to.

"You left me." Her voice deflated. "You said we would make it work, and then you left me, and I never heard from you again." The pain in her voice stabbed him through the chest.

She wasn't wrong. But he had spent the last twelve years thinking she'd moved on and basically left *him*. "You wrote to me that you'd found someone else."

She jerked free while he had a moment of weakness. And then she turned around to face him. Her eyes were heated and wide. "That was a matter of self-preservation, Mike." She stomped back toward the house.

Again, she'd left him staring at her back in shocked confusion. Finally, he took off after her, catching up as she slid the back door open and stepped inside. She kept going, but he grabbed her arm and spun her around. "Stop running from me."

She glanced down at the spot where his hand was wrapped around her biceps. "Stop touching me."

He released her, but only because he wasn't an asshole.

Luckily she didn't leave the room. She cocked a hip out and crossed her arms. Her face told him she was fighting tears. Again. Why did he always seem to make her cry? Was it possible she was still emotional enough about their breakup to shed tears over him? That was ludicrous.

Or maybe it wasn't. If he was perfectly honest, he could almost do the same. He shook his head. "Are you telling me you lied? You never met another man and had a new boyfriend?"

"That's what I'm telling you, big guy."

He took a step back, afraid he might actually fall. Her words shook his very foundation. He'd never once considered that possibility. "Why?"

"I told you. Self-preservation. You cut me off. You never responded to a single email I sent. I needed to do something. My father—"

"Whoa, wait," he cut her off to say, "your father? What did he have to do with this?"

She lowered her shoulders, blowing out a long breath. "He advised me to do it. He thought it would help me find closure, put an end to that chapter of my life."

"He advised you to lie to me?"

She narrowed her gaze. "What the hell did you care? You hadn't made contact with me since...since..." She didn't finish.

He knew exactly when the last time he'd spoken to her was. The night he'd taken her virginity and given her his. He lifted a hand to run it through his hair. Holy shit. Her dad told her to make up a boyfriend? Who did that?

Silence filled the room. Nothing except their collective

labored breathing. He had no idea how to respond. There was no way in hell he could tell her why he hadn't contacted her. Ever. She would hate him.

Suddenly he wondered how her dad had reacted to the news that it was Mike who would be picking her up and keeping her safe. Or shit. Maybe he didn't know…

Mike grabbed a kitchen chair and lowered onto it. He set his elbows on his knees and his forehead on his palms. What a shitstorm.

Zola didn't move. "That's it? You don't have anything else to say?"

"I have lots of things to say," he told the floor. "But none of them are going to make you feel better. I'm sorry. I didn't know."

"You're sorry." Her voice was sarcastic as hell. She tapped a foot to go with her stance.

"Yeah."

"Me too." She turned around and left the room.

And he let her go because he had no idea what else to do at that point.

Chapter Six

ZOLA WAS STARING out the bedroom window at the skyline when a knock sounded on the door and then opened. "Can I come in?"

She didn't respond. In fact, she continued to stare out the window.

When he got close enough to touch her, she stiffened and pointed to the window sill. "Your friend is really into safety." There were glass sensors all through the house.

"Yeah. He is. But then again, he does some seriously scary shit for the military and sometimes the government, so he has earned a certain level of paranoia. That's partly why I chose to bring you here instead of someplace else. We might not stay forever, but it was the safest place I knew where we could regroup and make another plan."

She turned around and leaned against the window sill. "We better do that then. Unless you want to back out and get someone else to play bodyguard."

"Not a chance, babe." He tucked his hands in his pockets and nodded toward the door. "Come bump heads with me. I need to show you a few things."

She passed him and made her way back to the kitchen where they'd been seated at his computer before the subject changed to how damn hot he made her when his skin touched hers. As an olive branch, she even intentionally pulled her chair right up to his before he sat.

She had no idea why he had ghosted her all those years ago, but obviously he had no intention of telling her, so she needed to make the best of this situation.

Mike slid into the seat next to her and grabbed the mouse. He clicked on several things and then opened a document that said it was six pages long.

"What's this?"

"A list of the threats to your life. If you want, I can show you the list of threats to your father's life also." He lifted a brow, glancing her direction.

Her jaw fell. "Where did you get that?"

"The CIA. They didn't hire me and then leave me hanging with no info."

"But I've never seen this list." She reached across him, knocked his hand out of the way, and took over his mouse to scan down the pages.

He leaned back enough to give her space, but his breath landed on her cheek. She had to ignore that detail. "Shit."

"Yeah."

"Why wasn't I informed?" She twisted to look at him, a mistake at such a short distance.

He shrugged. "No idea. Maybe your father was trying to protect you?"

She rolled her eyes. "He would do that."

"You're a grown adult. I can't believe he still manipulates you like that."

She pursed her lips and returned to face the screen. So many incidences of letters, emails, even attempted break-ins.

When she sat back, she addressed his statement. "He still sees me as a child."

"Apparently. Is that why you aren't married? Has no one ever been good enough for you in his eyes?"

She should have taken offense. If any other person had said those words to her, she would have flipped out. But Mike had a special pass. He knew her father. And he wasn't poking at her to be mean. He was seriously curious.

"I don't share my dating life with my father anymore, if that's what you're asking. The reason I'm not married is because no one has ever been good enough for me in *my* eyes." Maybe that was saying too much, but she didn't want him to think her father was still meddling in her life. At least not in that area.

He searched her gaze, apparently satisfied with her response.

"What about you? Why aren't you married?"

"The only woman who ever made me consider marriage left me for another man." He didn't hesitate to tell her that.

"Oh. Shit. That's awful. I'm sorry."

He stared at her hard.

She jerked backward. "You're not talking about me."

"I am."

She shoved the chair back again and stood, spinning

away from him exactly how she'd done earlier that morning. "Mike. That's crazy."

"Is it? Crazier than you making up a fake boyfriend to get me to leave you alone?"

Her face heated. "That is not what happened. *You* started it by ignoring my emails." Her voice rose completely out of her control. "I sent you that email to light a fire under you. It was my last-ditch effort to get you to come after me. You failed." Why the hell did she tell him that?

He stood as quickly as she had and took a step toward her.

She backed up as he approached until her butt hit the glass door.

He kept coming, stopping inches from her, his hands landing on the glass on both sides of her head. His gaze darted back and forth between her eyes, searching.

She couldn't breathe. Every inhale filled her with his scent. If she thought she could get away with it, she would close her eyes to block out at least the sight of him.

"We both miscalculated."

She shook her head. She wouldn't allow him to put equal blame on her. "No. Because I sent you five emails. *Five.*" She held up one hand, all fingers extended. "You sent me nothing. Not. One. Word."

He nodded sharply. "Fine. My bad. You're right. I should've written back."

Was it that easy? Did he seriously just take the blame? "Why?" A tear slid down her face, though she really wished it hadn't. Damn emotions.

"I thought it was better for you. Tidier. I thought I

needed to let you go."

She grabbed his shirt, unable to stop herself. She fisted the material of his tight tee in her hands, her voice increasing as she spoke again. "Bullshit. You coward. I loved you." Her voice quivered. Dammit. She shook him. Except he didn't budge. But she shook his shirt. "I loved you, you idiot. And you walked away from me without a word."

"I was wrong." He closed the distance, smashing his firm body into hers, flattening her to the window. The glass was cold. She welcomed the coolness against her heated body.

Another tear slid down to match the first.

Mike cupped her face with one hand and rubbed the wetness with the pad of his thumb. "I was wrong," he whispered again. "So very wrong."

More tears. Damn him.

And then his mouth was on hers.

She couldn't stop the rush of adrenaline that forced her to angle her head to the side and let him in.

His kiss was firm. Demanding. Like a starving man who hadn't eaten in days and then came upon a buffet. He threaded his other hand in her hair, still holding her face with the first hand. His tongue danced with hers, demanding everything.

Unable to stop herself, she gave him everything back. Every emotion she'd ever felt for him leaked into that kiss. She eased her fists open and smoothed her hands around to his back as he pressed into her farther.

Totally aware of his erection against her belly, wetness

leaked from her to soak her panties. She wanted him. Worse than she'd ever wanted anyone. Worse than she'd wanted him the first time he claimed her.

It infuriated her to so easily succumb to his touch, his lips, his wandering hands, his thick erection pressing against her… But she recognized it for what it was. Lust. Pure and simple. Nothing more.

Forever he kissed her, until her brain was scrambled and she knew nothing but being one with this man. When he finally eased back, he did so to nibble a path to her ear.

His lips against her sensitive skin sent a shudder down her body. Every time he'd done that in high school, she'd melted for him. Nothing had changed. "I loved you too, baby. So much it hurt. I'm sorry."

She still didn't understand why he'd left her. He'd carefully avoided that detail, but she didn't want to argue with him anymore today. Instead, she held on tighter, hugging him against her in response. Hoping she conveyed at least a truce.

When he set his teeth gently on her earlobe, she moaned. "God, I missed this," he whispered, his breath making her shiver in response.

It was like no time had passed. How was that possible?

"Now what do we do?" she finally asked his chest as she set her forehead against the rock-hard pec.

He lifted away from her ear, cupped her face, and forced her to meet his gaze, his body still pressed against hers. "Now, you take these threats seriously and help me figure out who this fucker is so we can stay one step ahead of him and keep you safe until he's behind bars."

She nodded. He was right. "Okay." She bit her lower lip, worrying it to match her fear. A very real fear she should have had yesterday and last week or even last month. Instead, she'd been kept out of the loop and lived in ignorance. She'd been cocky and unconcerned. "I don't understand why my father would do this. It wasn't safe keeping this information from me."

"Babe, he had people following you. Everywhere. But two days ago, the CIA decided that wasn't good enough."

"And they called you."

"Sort of. Like I said before, this arrangement is under the table. No one can pin anything back to the government. It's like I never existed. My job is to keep you alive while they figure out what to do."

She narrowed her gaze and smiled wanly. "Why do I get the feeling you aren't really a sit-back-and-wait sort of guy?"

He chuckled. "There's my girl. I knew you were in there somewhere." He kissed her soundly on the lips one more time and then released her to step back. His hands slid down to grasp hers. "Let's go sit on the couch. We can pour over the information and see if anything stands out to you."

She nodded. What stood out to her more than anything was the bulge in the front of his jeans, but she thought it might be better if she kept that thought to herself for the time being.

Two hours later, Zola was seriously stressed from all the information she'd absorbed. She pointed to a symbol that kept popping up on several pages. "What's this?"

"It's the calling card of a particular terrorist organization. One that likes to use biological warfare as their weapon of choice."

She gasped. "For real?"

"Yes."

"And that's why they called you. It's your specialty." As she realized this, it all made more sense.

She needed to call her dad, which had been niggling her in the back of her mind ever since that morning. She leaned back against the couch, closed her eyes, and rubbed her temples.

"Come here." He squeezed her thigh to get her attention. When she glanced at him, he had spread his knees and was pointing at the floor in front of him. "I'll rub your shoulders."

"Really?" she asked, lifting a brow. "That would be wonderful." She slid down to the floor and settled between his legs, leaning against the couch.

The second his hands began to knead her shoulders, she sighed. With expert fingers, he worked out each knot in her neck one by one. He was truly gifted with his hands.

She let her eyes close as the tension eased.

"You okay?" Mike asked from closer to her than she'd expected. He'd leaned his face down toward her ear.

"No. A terrorist organization is trying to hunt me down and kill me to get to my father. *And*," she added, opening her eyes and turning to face him, "I just found out that I still have the hots for my childhood sweetheart, which I've apparently carried around with me for twelve years."

She was being incredibly blunt with him, but after

twelve wasted years, why not throw everything in. Who cared? It wasn't like she intended to pick up where they left off. But the physical attraction was undeniable. That much had not changed in a dozen years.

Mike froze for a second, his hands still gripping her shoulders but his fingers not moving. And then he started again, working his way across her shoulders and down her biceps.

It occurred to her that he hadn't responded to her blatant statement, but then he took a deep breath and spoke, his hands never ceasing their work. "That fire never went out for me either, Zola."

Damn. Those words reached into her and started a slow burn. Parts of her body that had been dormant for over a decade came alive to tingle and torment her.

It would seem he was available. She was also available. They were trapped together for the foreseeable future. Her father could hardly do anything to sabotage it since he wasn't in the same state.

She was a grown woman who spent way too much time working, hardly dated, and never had sex. Mike was even sexier than he had been twelve years ago, and he made her panties damp. Oh, who was she kidding? She knew damn good and well he could make her body hum like she'd never permitted any other man to even attempt. Why not sleep with him? Maybe it would alleviate some of the stress or at least chase it to the corners of her mind for a while.

Mike reached for a lock of her hair and rubbed it between his fingers. "I always loved to thread my fingers in your hair." He leaned forward and set his nose against her ear, again.

She shivered. Again.

He whispered. Again. "You willing to explore this thing between us?"

"Mmm. I don't think I have a choice." She lifted a hand to cup the back of his neck, hoping she could lure his lips toward hers again. She should take this gift and sleep with him. If he was half as good a lover as he'd been twelve years ago, she'd be in heaven. It was just sex. Sex was good. Sex with Mike would be amazing. She deserved to let herself go and submerge herself in all that was Mike for a while.

That's all it could be. Nothing more. He'd hurt her. Badly. But that didn't mean she wasn't human. And damn she was attracted to him still.

It wasn't like she would ever do something like this with another man. Only Mike. He made her feel things no other man ever had or probably ever would.

She needed the release. All she had to do was compartmentalize and remind herself she was scratching an itch with a man she knew could rock her world. *Don't get emotional about this, Zola. Just do it.*

If they were going to be trapped in this beach house for the foreseeable future, she could let herself take advantage of whatever he was willing to offer.

But he pulled back, shocking her with his next words. "How about if I clean up this pizza mess from lunch earlier, and we get dressed and go out?"

"Out?" She twisted to stare up at him and lifted a brow.

"Yeah." He shrugged. "We could be on lockdown here

for a while. Let's slip out for a bit. Eat. Enjoy a normal meal."

That wasn't at all what she had in mind for the next hour. Once she set her mind on having another taste of Mike Dorsen, she really didn't want to leave the house and make nice in public.

Mike extricated himself from her and stood. He was chuckling as he picked up the empty box and soda cans.

"What's funny?" Maybe she shouldn't have asked, but she couldn't help herself.

"You truly have not changed," he said as he padded from the room to dispose of their trash.

"How so?" She hoisted herself off the floor and sat on the couch.

He returned and leaned over her, straddling her knees while setting his hands on the back of the couch. He lowered his face toward hers and kissed her nose. "You spent over a year trying to get me into bed with you when we were kids. And here you are doing it again."

Her face flushed for the tenth time that day. "Seriously? You act like I'm some kind of nymphomaniac who can't go without. I never said anything about having sex anyway. I'm just surprised you want to go out in public."

"Babe. Like I said, I don't know how long we might need to be diligent here, but this house is safe, the best place we can be while others work to gather information. It's not going to take too many days for whoever is after you to find us. So, yeah. Let's go to dinner before we lock ourselves in. You're going to be stuck with me." He waggled his eyebrows teasingly.

"Fine. You want to go out? We'll go out." She set her hands on his rock-hard chest and shoved him away. Game on.

MIKE WAS LEERY about her change in attitude. She had something up her sleeve, and he knew it wasn't going to work in his favor. She'd relented to go out a little too quickly. And the twinkle in her eyes said everything.

She floated through the room with her head held high and her shoulders back like the true debutante she was, and then she disappeared into her bedroom, shutting the door with a resounding snick.

Mike headed for his own bedroom and returned ten minutes later with his best jeans on, loafers, and a dark navy, button-down shirt. He hadn't said as much, but it was sort of a date, after all. He could at least dress to impress.

He needed to get her out of the tight quarters where the entire place had filled with her scent and her sweet, sexy body had driven him crazy for twenty-four hours. The last thing he wanted to do was presumptuously claim her body again so soon after clearing the air between them. Even though it seemed that was what she wanted from him.

Never mind that they'd known each other years ago. They were different people now. Grown. Adults. They had changed. Hadn't they?

He wasn't sure what her aim was. She melted a bit when he kissed her, and she also seemed a bit too willing to have sex. He hated to ponder the implications. When they'd been teenagers, she'd been the one pleading with him to take her virginity, so he shouldn't have been surprised. But they weren't teenagers anymore, and he was uncertain of her current motives. Something felt off.

A noise from the hall made him spin around. He stopped dead, grabbing the back of the couch to steady himself when she came into view.

Shit. He had played this card. It was entirely his fault. But who knew she would have brought along any clothing remotely resembling that dress to hide from a killer? "Jesus... Zola..." His voice was gravelly, his throat tight.

She glanced down. "What? Did I get something on me?" Her voice was coy. Teasing. Sultry. Sexy.

Fuck.

"Babe." He groaned. "I'm not going to sleep with you just because you wear a short skirt." It was so much more than a short skirt, and he knew it. That dress was the definition of sex. And she needed to take it off and pick something else before he came in his pants or had to fend off other patrons of the restaurant.

She smiled, or smirked again, sending him a wink. "You said we were going out. I presume you mean dinner. This is all I brought to go out in. I didn't imagine dinners and wine when we left the house yesterday."

"And yet, you packed that." His gaze roamed down her body slowly again. The cream-colored, tight-fitting material hugged every one of her assets perfectly. It hit only a few inches below her pussy, and he couldn't imagine how it might look from behind. If he saw it, he would probably choke. Her tits alone were enough to make any man salivate. And those fucking heels.

He took a deep breath. Fine. If she wanted to play this game, he would go along. But she was in for a world of hurt if she thought he would fuck her later simply because of a dress. It was just a dress after all.

Keep telling yourself that.

She turned around and headed for the kitchen table where her coat was draped over a chair.

Fuck me. He couldn't stop the groan that escaped his lips.

"Did you say something?"

He lifted a brow. He wanted to demand she change. But he knew she would find that amusing and dig her spiked heels in. Besides, would it really help if she squeezed her ass back into those fucking jeans and dragged a tight shirt over her breasts? No.

But the back of that dress… It mostly wasn't there. She had pulled her hair off her neck in a loose twist, and the back dipped so low that he could easily reach into the dip and touch her ass. Which also meant she wasn't wearing a bra.

As she crossed the room in his direction, she grabbed her purse off the couch and lifted it. "I did forget one thing though."

"What's that?"

"Matching clutch. My regular purse will have to do." She tossed him a grin. Of course she knew he couldn't possibly give a fuck what purse she carried, nor would he notice.

"Ready?" she asked.

"Yep." His voice was too high. And his cock was too tight behind the denim. It was going to be a long night.

He lifted his coat from a hook next to the front door and slid it on. After helping her into her own, he reset the alarm and opened the front door. The backpack he never left for any reason sat next to the door. He grabbed it and followed her out.

He led her outside to the SUV and opened the door, taking her hand to help her onto the seat. He had to grit his teeth as he got a glimpse way too high between her thighs. Luckily he didn't see what she wore under the dress. Or perhaps the reality was, the answer was nothing. In which case, he didn't want to know.

He drove them to the local strip mall where he'd seen a family-owned Italian restaurant. It was small and intimate, and he didn't think there was a chance in hell anyone knew where Zola was yet.

He had no doubt whoever wanted her would find her. Eventually. But not yet. He had covered their tracks as well as he could, paying for the plane with cash and then taking a circuitous route to the house when they arrived last night.

He wasn't stupid. Terrorists didn't play nice. They would find her. But hopefully Mike had enough intelligence working on things to have a heads-up that would buy them time to get the hell out of town.

For tonight, he thought they were safe.

When they arrived, he jumped down from the front seat and rounded the Tahoe fast enough to take Zola's hand and help her down also. And then he made the mistake of setting his hand on the small of her back under the edge of her jacket to guide her toward the entrance.

Her skin… So smooth and warm. And the heat from her sweet body raced through his arm and down to his cock. It was permanently stiff, but this wasn't helping.

He wasn't disappointed when they entered the restaurant. It was dimly lit, romantic, and not overly crowded.

"Two of you, sir?" the hostess asked.

"Yes, please."

She led them between the tables toward the back and seated them at a booth.

Mike held Zola's hand as she slid into the seat and then he nodded for her to keep scooting and slid in next to her instead of taking the bench across from her.

She ignored his seating choice or intentionally didn't say anything as she removed her coat and settled it against the wall. The front of her dress was cut low enough to give him an amazing view of her cleavage. Yep. It was going to be a long night.

In less than a minute, a waiter showed up. "Hi, I'm Vincent. Can I get you two anything to drink while you look at the menu?"

Zola was quick to answer. "I'll have your house red, please."

Hmm. She was a wine drinker. When they'd been in high school, she hadn't ever had a sip of alcohol, which meant he hadn't consumed much either. Sometimes he had a beer with friends at a party, but he rarely went out without her. It never interested him. Even after her father caught on to their games and barely let her leave the house, Mike still had little interest in partying while she sat at home.

"Sir?"

"I'll have whatever's on tap. Thank you."

"Never developed a taste for beer," she stated when the waiter wandered away.

He chuckled. "Not surprising."

"What's that supposed to mean?"

He was still teasing her when he turned to face her and continued with a shrug. "You aren't the sort of woman I can picture with a beer in hand is all. Don't try to make it something else."

She narrowed her gaze. "Everything with you was always something else."

"Now it's my turn to ask, what's that supposed to mean?"

She tapped the table with her perfectly groomed nails and said nothing.

Seconds ticked by. Mike licked his lips. "Let's not argue. Okay? We're out. It's a nice evening."

"Deal." She bent her head to peruse the menu.

The waiter showed up with their drinks two minutes later, took their orders, and left them.

Mike took a long swig of his beer and faced Zola. "Tell me about yourself. How did you end up with the DA?" His leg brushed against hers, and he held very still, absorbing her warmth while pretending he didn't notice.

She lit up. Good. She loved her job. He wasn't surprised. "The normal route. Four years of college. Two years of law school. Bar exams. A few unfulfilling jobs for law firms. And then I landed this job. It's not cushy. The pay is shit. But I love it." She leaned on her palm and her face remained passionate. Excited.

He couldn't keep from smiling at her.

"And you? How did you end up in the navy?"

"The normal route," he mimicked. "Four years of college. Then grad school. Two years with the navy. SEAL exams. I skipped the unfulfilling jobs though and went straight to the Middle East. Did two tours. Got shot. Discharged. Went to work for the FBI."

"Doing what?"

"I'm a biologist. I take on whatever assignment they hand me and usually spend most of my time in a lab solving the crime. I just spent over a year in Chicago. I was exhausted and took a leave of absence to regroup."

"And then you got this job."

"And then I got this job," he repeated.

"Coincidence?"

"Is there such a thing?" he asked.

Her smile grew wider.

Their food arrived, and they spent the next half hour enjoying one of the best meals he'd had in a long time. Take out and cold sandwiches were his norm.

Occasionally their arms brushed against each other. He noticed her goosebumps but said nothing.

When she finished her meal, she turned toward him again, sipping her second glass of wine. "I feel like I've slipped into another dimension."

He spun his beer glass in circles. "Yeah. It's surreal. I never expected to see you again."

Her face fell into that sad place again.

He quickly spoke to do damage repair. "Let's not dwell on the past, okay? We can't change it. All we can do is move forward." The last thing he wanted to do was rehash their separation. Ever.

She nodded, taking another sip of her wine. She didn't look convinced, nor did she make eye contact with him at the suggestion.

In his rational mind, he knew he would eventually be forced to face what happened, but if he could put it off indefinitely, he would.

Was it fair? Probably not. But he intended to do it anyway. If he dumped shit that would royally piss her off at her feet, there was a good chance she would be angry enough to send him packing. And then someone else would have to step in and protect her.

The reality was he didn't trust another man with her life. He wasn't willing to take that risk. No way in hell could he turn the task over to someone else and walk away. He wouldn't be able to sleep at night worrying about her safety and thinking about her sexy body.

It was too late to turn back the clock now. They were in this. And he needed to see it through to completion. After the terrorists were apprehended, he would sit her down and dish out the ugly facts, but not before. Too risky.

His feelings for her hadn't changed in twelve years. So no. He wouldn't risk her wrath or her safety. Not for anything in the world.

Of course, that also meant he would be a jackass to sleep with her. He could move forward with the best of intentions. But he knew from experience she was relentless when it came to getting in his pants. She'd managed before, and she would do so again. Today? Tomorrow? Next week?

He had no idea how long he could fend off her advances. The fact that he didn't want to made it even harder. It was his own fault for opening this door. He could have kept his hands to himself and put her off. Instead, he'd not only touched her but then gave her a massage on top of things. But he would feel like a dick if he slept with her while knowingly withholding details about their breakup.

Hurting her was the last thing he ever wanted to do, but it was inevitable. The question was: Could she forgive him? Was there even a remote possibility they could start over?

He shook the thought from his mind. She would never forgive him for letting her go. And she shouldn't. He deserved it. Did it mean they couldn't sleep together? Out of mutual attraction? It was just sex. Not a commitment.

They sat in silence for several moments.

Just as Mike finished his beer and set the glass on the table, intent on flagging down the waiter for the bill, his phone vibrated in his pocket.

It was late. Not that he didn't get calls at all hours of the day and night, but he never ignored a call, even after regular business hours.

"Is that your phone?" she asked.

"Yeah." He pulled it out of his pocket and read the text.

Tex: *Where are you? Call me. Now.*

"Shit," he muttered as he hit the button to connect

with Tex.

"What is it?" she asked.

He met her gaze while the line connected. "No idea. Can't be good."

Tex answered in one ring. "Mike. Where are you?"

"Italian restaurant. The one in the strip about a mile north of your house."

"Yeah, I know the place. Listen, you've been compromised."

"Fuck. How do you know?" He glanced around, lowering his voice.

Zola set her hand on his arm. He wrapped his fingers around hers and faced her, knowing the look on his face was not pretty.

"Got a notification that security at the house had been breached. Been watching it for about a minute. Two men. Black clothes. Spotted them in every outdoor camera. They checked every window and door and then hid in the bushes."

"Fuck," Mike repeated, probably too loudly. He yanked out his wallet, pulled out more than enough money to cover the bill, and dropped it on the table. Next, he pointed to Zola's coat and mouthed, "Put your coat on, babe."

He slid out of the booth, yanking on his own jacket, reengaging with Tex. "Give me two seconds. Hang on."

"You got it."

Mike wrapped his arm around a very nervous Zola and looked around before leading her to the front door and rushing her toward the Tahoe. He held up a finger to stop her from getting too close and glanced around the car before finally disengaging the locks.

Somewhat satisfied it hadn't been tampered with, he led her to the driver's side, still holding the phone to his ear. "Gonna start the car, Tex. You still with me?"

"Yep."

Mike looked at Zola. "Stand back a few feet, babe. Let me start it before we get in." He knew it wasn't logical. If the car was compromised, they were too close to it to survive an explosion anyway, but he didn't have many choices. He wasn't about to let her out of his sight. He couldn't very well start the engine without reaching inside. And there was only a small chance anyone had followed them to the restaurant.

More than likely the men at the house had gotten there after Mike and Zola left, especially since it sounded as though they were now lying in wait.

The engine started without a problem, and Mike sat halfway in the SUV to put it in drive and then back into park. Satisfied it wasn't strapped with explosives, he left it running, jumped back down, and took Zola's hand to lead her to the passenger side.

Two seconds later, she was safely buckled in, and he was in his own seat, setting the cell phone down as it engaged with the blue tooth. "Tex. I'm back. You're on speaker. We're on the move."

"Good. Hi, Zola. Nice to meet you. Sorry it's under duress." His voice changed back to serious. "Mike, I don't have to tell you the obvious."

"Of course not. Heading west. I'll jump on the highway in a few minutes." No way could they return to the house.

"What's happening?" Zola finally asked, her voice a bit too high. "Did they find us? I assume they're at the house?"

"Yeah." Mike maneuvered the car onto the interstate. "I'm sorry. I thought we had more time. I never would have taken the risk of going to dinner if I thought someone was that close on our heels."

"Gonna point out the obvious again, buddy," Tex stated. "If you had been in the house, you would probably be in a far bigger bind than you are now."

"True." Mike picked up speed, glancing out the rearview mirror every few seconds. He gripped the steering wheel so tight his knuckles hurt.

Zola reached across the console and set a hand on his thigh, giving it a squeeze.

He returned the support by grasping her fingers for a moment. But then he needed his hand on the steering wheel. "Can't tell you how glad I am to have rented your house, man," he said to Tex.

"That was convenient. But I'm sorry to say, I don't have homes all over the country with surveillance set up." He chuckled. "You're on your own now. Call your contact and let him know about those two goons. I doubt they'll hang around long though."

"Right. I'll catch up with you later. Thanks again." Mike ended the call and grabbed his cell to tap the screen and engage another number.

Two rings later, he had Greg Lambert on the phone. "Dorsen."

"Got a problem."

"Talk to me."

"Two men are at the house. We weren't there at the time. We're also not returning."

"Got it. Let me get a team over there. I'll get back with you." Lambert ended the call without another word.

Zola's hand slid away, and she tucked her fingers between her legs.

"You cold?" He reached for the dials to fiddle with the temperature.

"No." She turned her head toward the window. She was scared. Processing. Freaking out probably.

He couldn't blame her. She should be. If she'd had any reserved complacency about this situation lingering in her mind, it was erased now. "Gonna get us a safe distance away and then find a hotel."

"'Kay." She turned toward him. "Who was the second man you spoke to?"

He glanced at her. "My contact with the CIA."

"You can't tell me who it is," she mumbled.

"Right." His chest tightened. There was nothing he could do to console her at the moment. He needed to drive and pay attention to his surroundings. He was certain no one followed them, but he wasn't taking any chances.

He decided to head north, circling the major cities while working their way back toward Connecticut over several days. Something didn't sit right, and he thought it was a bad idea to be too far away. His gut said to meander back toward Connecticut.

She was shivering, so he turned up the heat coming

from under the dash on her side of the car. Her legs were bare. And now wasn't the time to pay close attention to that fact. Sexy as he knew they were, terrorists were after them.

After a long time, she started asking questions. "Do you think they want to kidnap me for ransom or something?"

"I don't know, babe." He truly didn't. And he kept his voice calm.

"What good would it do to kill me? That wouldn't get my father off their backs. It would infuriate him."

"True. Unless..." Should he point out the thought niggling in the back of his mind?

"What?" She spun to face him.

He glanced at her wide eyes. "Maybe this has nothing to do with your father at all and everything to do with one of the cases you tried."

She chewed on her lower lip for a moment and then nodded. "Shit. Maybe you're right."

"However," he continued, "if that were the reason, then the case is probably over. What good would it do to kidnap you now? None of the current cases you're working on concern terrorist attacks. I went through all of them earlier. You've been on five cases that were related to terrorism. Of those, three were convicted."

"Maybe they want to kidnap me and hold me until the felon is released?"

"Possible. Not likely. They could kidnap anyone if that were the case. Or an entire building of people. It happens all the time. No need to specifically go after the DA or the assistant DA."

She slumped in the seat.

"I'm going to get off at the next exit and find us a place to stay."

"Okay."

Chapter Seven

ZOLA WAS EXHAUSTED when they reached the hotel. She wished she could have slept in the car, but every time she closed her eyes, she pictured two men in dark clothes lurking around the fantastic beach home that didn't even belong to them.

She hoped those two assholes didn't do anything to destroy the house, because it was gorgeous and owned by Mike's friend. The man was kind enough to let Mike stay in it. He hadn't known it would be compromised by terrorists when he rented it out.

Now what? She had no idea what the plan was, and honestly, she couldn't focus on anything except fear for more than a few seconds at a time.

She tugged her coat around her shoulders and crossed her arms in front of her as if she were chilled to the bone as they headed for the hotel entrance. Mike set his hand on her back to lead her, and the heat of his palm seemed to reach through her coat. Irrational, but it soothed her.

She hardly paid any attention to whatever he said to the

man behind the desk as he secured a room, and then they were in the elevator. "I have nothing," she mumbled, as if that mattered when she should be grateful she was alive.

"I know. We'll get some things. Don't worry."

She pointed at his back pack. "What's in there? And why did you bring it with us?"

He hauled it farther up his shoulder. "I don't go any-where without at least my backpack. It's rare for me to even leave it in the car. I hate that I was complacent enough to have done that. But I'm glad I grabbed it from the house."

"You didn't answer my question," she pointed out as they stepped out of the elevator.

He gave her a wry smile. "Mostly you don't want to know. Weapons. Money. Important stuff like that."

"So no toothbrushes? Shampoo? Important stuff like that?" She tried to mimic him as if the two lists were similar. And she tried to sound humorous.

He chuckled. "No. Sorry." His hand again at the small of her back, he led her to the room and opened the door.

Instant heat hit her in the face. It was too hot in the room. But under the circumstances, she was so cold, it felt welcome. She kicked off her heels, shrugged out of her coat, and draped it over the back of a chair while Mike turned the deadbolt and slid the chain through its channel.

Without a word, he reached for the thermostat to ad-just it next. And then he passed her up to drag the blinds closed, dropped his own jacket on top of hers, and came to her. The look on his face made her unravel. She pursed her lips to hold her emotions in an attempt to prevent tears of stress from falling. "Shit," she muttered against his chest as he tugged her in for a hug.

He threaded one hand into her hair, set the other on the bare skin of her back, and stroked her gently. "We're safe now."

"Are we?" she asked his dress shirt. It didn't seem like she was safe. In fact, it seemed like she hadn't been safe for a long time. She'd been in denial.

"Shh. Baby, we are. Trust me. No one followed us here. We won't stay more than the night, but you can relax for now."

She nodded against him, words no longer possible. After an intense hour in the car with her mind wandering to every possible and impossible scenario, she felt wrung out.

Mike continued to hold her, rocking her gently in his embrace.

She slowly relaxed, turning her face to one side so that her cheek rested on his firm pecs. There was one bed in the room. King-size. Maybe in another time or place she would have cared about that arrangement but not in this new world. No way would she want to sleep any place but in his arms.

He wouldn't balk at the idea, would he?

She took a deep breath, and Mike slid his hands to her face to cup her cheeks and tip her head back. "Better?"

"Yeah."

A knock sounded at the door, and she nearly jumped out of her skin.

"Sorry. My bad. I forgot to mention someone was bringing us a few necessities."

"Ah." She hated the loss the second he released her to head for the door. As if still chilled, she crossed her arms and shuddered while he looked through the peephole and then opened the door to take a bag of items from house-keeping.

After securing them inside again, he turned around. "Toothpaste. Toothbrushes. Razors. Comb. Maybe not everything you'd normally use, but better than nothing." He reached into the tiny bathroom and set the stash on the counter. And then he was back. His brow furrowed.

She took a deep breath. "I'll be okay." She forced herself to straighten to her full height and pulled her shoulders back. She didn't drop her arms, but it was all she could do.

He set his hands on her shoulders and met her gaze. "What can I do?"

"Honestly?"

He nodded, his eyes narrowing. "Of course."

The world was upside down. Her entire existence was precarious. She was trapped in a small hotel room with the only man she'd ever loved. She didn't have the first clue why he let her walk away all those years ago, but at the moment, she also didn't care.

Her attraction to him hadn't lessened with time. And it would appear he still desired her also. So, what did she need? She needed the connection she knew they still shared.

"I need you to make love to me." She'd been open about sex even at seventeen. He had also turned her down repeatedly at that time. If he did so now, she might actually come undone.

They were grown adults, not kids. She wasn't a virgin.

Her father didn't rule her life any longer. They weren't strangers.

And yet, he didn't respond in a way she wanted. "I don't think that's a good idea."

She groaned. Her shoulders fell, and she wiggled out of his grasp. "Seriously? What are you? Twelve?" She ducked around him to get to the bathroom, where at least she wouldn't have to look at him.

"Zola…"

She grabbed the doorframe and looked back at him. "Do you not realize how insulting that is to a woman? That's not the first time I've put all my cards on the table only to have you turn me down. It hurts. But don't worry. It won't happen again. That's the last time I'll open myself up to that level of vulnerability." She slid into the bathroom, shut the door, and locked it.

Mike's expression had been one of shock, his eyes wide, his hands fisted at his sides.

She turned on the shower before doing anything else and then eased out of the only item of clothing she had with her and hooked it behind the door. Under the sound of the water running, she groaned. She didn't even have on panties or a bra.

Regardless of the unintended outcome of the evening, she had worn that dress without a bra or panties intentionally to seduce Mike after dinner. She'd wanted to tease him, maybe coax some answers out of him. If things had gone her way, she had been open to the possibility of sleeping with him. Damn the consequences. And the intensity of the night hadn't dampened that need.

The bathroom filled with steam, so she stepped under the spray and closed the curtain. For a long time, she stood there, letting the water run down her body, warming her, loosening her muscles. She was wrinkly by the time she grabbed the hotel shampoo, conditioner, and then soap.

When she finally stepped out of the enclosure, she made use of everything else Mike had acquired, grateful for his thoughtfulness while still pissed at his overly chivalrous stance.

"I'm not a goddamn child," she muttered. "I know my mind." With a deep breath, she turned around, grabbed a dry towel, and wrapped it around her. She didn't have a thing to wear. Not even panties. Too damn bad.

When she opened the door, she almost dropped the grip she had on the towel and swallowed her tongue.

Mike stood in the doorway, two inches from her, his hands holding the frame. He was also completely naked. "Do I look twelve to you?"

She swallowed. No. No, he certainly did not. Had he been that damn big in high school? She let her gaze roam up and down his body, pausing a moment at his left knee, the one that had obviously undergone several surgeries and had scars on both sides. The injuries only made him sexier somehow. Like badges of honor. Courage.

He released the doorframe slowly and reached out to grab the corner of the towel where she held it together. With a quick yank, he divested her of the barrier and dropped it on the floor.

His gaze heated as he perused her body. "*You* certainly don't look twelve."

It took every ounce of self-control not to cover herself. Instead, she let him look. After all, she had yet to remove her gaze from his chiseled body either.

"You were the hottest girl in school, but so much better now as a woman."

Her face heated at the compliment.

He lifted a hand again and gently, slowly stroked a finger down her cheek, across her neck, over her shoulder, and then between her breasts.

She shuddered.

He didn't stop there. He circled her breast and then slid that finger right over the tip of her nipple.

She moaned, arching her chest toward him.

"Oh, baby. That's so fucking sexy." He lurched forward, wrapped his arm around her, and hauled her against him. In less than a second, soft was gone and hard took over. He crushed her against his hard body and took her lips in a kiss that drove all thoughts away.

Sliding one arm under her ass, he lifted her and carried her to the bed. Without breaking the kiss, he lowered her back to the mattress and came down over her.

Every nerve ending tingled all over her body. She needed more, so she grasped at him, digging her fingers into his back. She let her tongue reach into his mouth to taste him. More. She was so hot. So aroused.

He shoved a knee between her legs, forcing them apart. If it bothered him to prop himself up on his bad knee, he gave no indication.

She lifted her sex up to meet his thigh, grinding her clit against him.

He threaded one hand in the hair at the back of her head and held her steady while his other hand trailed down her body to cover her breast and mold it in his palm.

She moaned. Or he did. Or they both did.

He bit her lip and sucked it into his mouth before finally breaking the kiss to continue nibbling her mouth and then across her cheek.

She gasped for breath while he tugged her hair, forcing her head to one side so he could gain access to her ear. When his lips landed on that sensitive spot, he exhaled.

She shuddered, her hands trailing down his back to clasp his ass. Damn, he was solid. Even his butt was rock-hard.

"You're sure?" he whispered in her ear.

"Jesus, Mike. Yes." Her voice was breathy. Low. Not her own.

He licked her earlobe lightly. "You. Are. So. Hot." He kissed her neck between each word.

Chills became goosebumps.

She squirmed, squeezing his ass in attempt to get better purchase against his thigh. Every inch of her sex was wet and pleading for release.

"Mike…"

"Gonna take my time, baby. Don't rush me."

She sighed. Arguing with him would be futile.

He scooted lower on the bed, his leg dislodging from her clit. When his face was at the same level as her chest, he lifted onto his elbows and stared at her breasts. His gaze darted back and forth. "Been wanting to see these since the moment you opened the front door to me yesterday."

She bit the corner of her lower lip and held it.

Watching him watch her was so arousing.

When he lowered his mouth to lick her nipple, she released her lip to gasp. So good. So damn good she thought she might come from that one lick.

But she didn't, and she was immediately distracted when he sucked her nipple into his mouth and flicked his tongue over the distended tip. "Oh. God."

He switched to give the other breast the same treatment, leaving behind a swollen wet nipple that tightened further as the air hit it.

When he was seemingly satisfied with her breasts, he scooted farther and nuzzled her belly. "You smell so good. The weird hotel soap can't mask your scent."

She held his shoulders now. Gripped them, her fingers digging into his skin. He would have half-moon circles from her nails all over his body. "Mike…" Her legs were stretched open to accommodate his enormous body, and when she realized he intended to continue exploring farther south, she stiffened. "Mike," she repeated. "Please. I need you inside me."

"You'll have me, baby. In a minute," he murmured. He kissed a path to her thigh and then switched to the inside of the other one. When his hands grasped her above the knees and spread her wider, she moaned.

"Mike, don't… I mean…" Was he going to kiss her there? She wasn't ready for that.

He hesitated only long enough to stare at her open sex and then flicked his tongue across her clit.

She screamed out sharply. It felt so good she almost

didn't care that his face was *there*.

"Jesus, baby. You're so responsive." He licked her slower the second time, and then closed his mouth over her clit and sucked gently.

She tipped her head back. Her vision swam as she got close to the edge of orgasm. He had definitely not done this to her the first time they'd had sex. He had looked. He had touched. He had not sucked.

She let go of his head to grab at the sheet at her sides, bracing herself for the orgasm that was so close.

Did he realize she was on the edge and had he intentionally backed off every time she almost tipped over? How could he know?

Suddenly his lips were around her clit again, sucking harder. And he thrust a finger into her tight channel.

She pressed her heels hard into the mattress and called out his name as her orgasm washed through her body. Her sex pulsed around his finger and his mouth. And he continued to suckle her, his finger thrusting in and out.

When it was over, he didn't stop. She squirmed under his touch. "Too sensitive," she whispered.

He hummed against her sex and only let up the slightest bit.

She wanted him inside her.

He seemed content to continue torturing her, which was exactly what happened as her body climbed that path to full arousal again. As if she'd been on a roller coaster and had reached the peak and then fallen down the other side. Exhilarating, but then the coaster climbed the next hill. Slowly.

Before she reached the top and tipped over the edge again, Mike released her clit. He wiped her moisture from his mouth with his hand and then slowly crawled up her body, keeping his finger inside her. "Baby, you are so damn tight. It's as if you haven't had sex since the last time I was with you."

She held her breath, forcing herself to concentrate on how good it felt for him to stroke the inside of her channel. She knew she was flushed, but it was already there from sex.

Mike kissed her nipples again, his body sliding to the side of hers so that one knee remained nestled between her legs and his hand could still explore her.

"Mike…" How long was he going to wait?

"Mmm."

She lowered her gaze to find him watching her face.

"I could do this all night." His languid torture continued. Finally, he added a finger.

She sucked in a sharp breath at the stretch.

"Zola. God." His hand slid out, and he leaned across her body to reach for something. A second later, he was on his knees beside her rolling on a condom. And then he climbed between her legs again. "You sure?"

She grabbed his arms and tugged. "Enough altruism, Mike."

He chuckled briefly before sobering again and lowering himself between her legs. He lined his length up with her entrance and rubbed her with the tip. Lodged in just the right spot, he released his hold and drew his arms up to rest on his elbows, looking down at her.

She whimpered. What was he waiting for?

He slowly slid inside, holding her gaze, watching her intently.

And it felt so very right. Perfect. Everything about this connection was exactly as she fantasized. It was tight. There was a moment of stretch, but she ignored it and waited out the twinge until nothing was left but pleasure.

Raw pleasure.

The best experience of her life hands down. Even better than the last time they'd had sex.

In slow motion, he eased in and out of her, going deeper each time. His gaze never left her. It seemed he could see into her soul. And maybe he could.

His lips were tight as if he was holding back. Also probably true.

"So…" He thrust into her. "Damn…" He pulled almost out. "Tight…" He thrust in again. And then, as if he lost the ability to see properly, he lowered his face to the side of hers and continued to pump in and out while he spoke into her ear. "So sexy… You have no idea…"

She had some idea, based on his expression.

Then he was fully seated, the base of him rubbing her clit with every pass.

She lifted into each thrust, giving herself a better angle.

He burrowed his hand into her hair, his palm resting on the side of her face. And he gripped her, perhaps without realizing it. "I want you to come with me, baby," he whispered into her ear.

If there was any doubt about that possibility, it dispelled the moment he spoke.

He released her face to lower his hand down her body,

grazing her breast before reaching between them to set his thumb on her clit.

"Oh. God… Mike." She grabbed his butt with both hands, holding him closer, wanting him deeper. She wanted him to crawl inside her and stay.

He stroked her clit.

She came. Hard. Fast. It swept through her unexpectedly.

Before she stopped pulsing, Mike thrust deep one last time and grunted out his own release. His body jerked with his orgasm.

She enjoyed the pressure of him over her and the way her clit was swollen and sensitive against his groin.

His breathing was heavy when he began to relax. Of course, hers was still labored too. And her ears were ringing as if she was under water. It took several minutes to catch her breath.

When he slid out, he lifted his face to smile. "Don't move."

She couldn't move if she wanted to, but why? She watched him pad across the room to the bathroom. He didn't close the door, but the water ran, and then he was back with a washcloth in his hand.

She realized his intention and reached out a hand.

He frowned in return. "Let me." And then he pressed her legs open wider and wiped away the wetness with the warm cloth. After he dropped it on the floor, he climbed up next to her again and propped himself on his side, staring down at her. He tossed one leg over hers and set his hand on her belly, his thumb grazing the underside of her breast.

She met his gaze, feeling dazed and a little self-conscious now that the intensity had passed.

"You're an amazing woman, Zola Carver."

"You're pretty awesome yourself, Mike Dorsen." She smiled.

He watched her face for a long time and then leaned over to turn off the light. He dragged the comforter over their bodies and turned her on her side so that her back nestled against his front.

It felt so good having him hold her like that. No comparison in the world. He had no idea what this meant to her. How huge this was. Monumental.

She needed to get a grip on her emotions. It was just sex. Nothing more. She kept telling herself that.

He stroked her belly for a while, kissing her neck. And then he spoke the dreaded words she had hoped to avoid. "I have never felt a woman that tight around me, Zola. How damn long has it been since you had sex?"

She stopped breathing. Did they have to go there? Now?

"Zola?" He froze, his fingers gripping the skin under her breast, holding her tighter.

There was no way to avoid this, so she whispered the words that would rock his world. "You were there."

He didn't move. In fact, he stopped breathing.

Seconds ticked by. Too many of them. She grew nervous. What was he thinking?

Finally, he released her, shot to sitting, and turned the light back on. He grabbed her chin and forced her gaze to meet his as she rolled onto her back. "Tell me you're kidding."

She bit her lip, a renewed flush rushing across her face. Her heart pounded.

He stared at her, his brow furrowed as if he was angry. Was he? And then he groaned, his face tipping toward the ceiling. His hand still held her chin. When he jerked his gaze back toward her, he finally spoke again. "Why? Why, Zola? I don't get it."

She shrugged, clearing her throat. "I never met someone who made me feel like you did. There was no comparison. I wasn't willing to settle for less." Years of pent-up words flowed out like hot lava. "Why would I have sex with someone who didn't set me on fire? There was no sense in it."

He was breathing heavily. His eyes were still drawn together. He stared at her, holding her gaze intently. When he licked his lips, she licked hers. "I don't even know what to say."

"It's okay. I know it's shocking. Kind of embarrassing really. I've never told anyone."

He shook his head, a few hard jerks. "No. Baby. God. Don't be embarrassed. I've never received a gift like this before. I never dreamed… I thought…"

"I know. My fault. You thought I was with someone else. I get it."

He swallowed. "But even after… I mean yesterday. I mean just because you lied in that email didn't give me any indication that you'd *never* slept with someone else." He was shaking.

She grabbed his wrist at her chin, squeezing. "I'm sorry," she felt compelled to whisper.

"Don't be sorry." He groaned. "I'm a dick."

"Don't go there, Mike."

"It's like I just took your virginity all over again."

"So? I asked for it. Begged. Pleaded. Just like I did the first time." She smiled, attempting to lighten the mood.

"I would have been gentler. Slower. Careful. Why didn't you say something?"

She rose to sitting next to him. She cupped his face in her hands and brought her lips to his for a brief kiss. "You couldn't have been gentler or slower or more careful, Mike. You were perfect. And I didn't want you to treat me with kid gloves. I wanted you to make love to me."

Seconds ticked by again before he finally snapped out of it and grabbed her around the waist to pull her closer. He flattened their chests together awkwardly and kissed a line across her shoulder and neck and cheek until his lips met hers and he slid his tongue inside.

This kiss was different. It wasn't urgent, but it was demanding. It was filled with gratitude and affection. It was sweet and endearing.

When he finally released her swollen lips, he set his forehead against hers and stared at her some more. "I will never forget this, Zola."

She jerked free of him, shaking her head. "Don't. God, Mike. Don't say that."

He looked confused, his eyes narrowed. "What did I say? What's wrong?"

"That's the exact same thing you said to me the last time I saw you. And then you left and never came back."

She fought against the onslaught of emotion that brought tears to her eyes.

He groaned. "I'm so sorry. It won't happen again. Not this time."

What did he even mean? That he wouldn't leave? That was ludicrous. Of course he would leave. He had a job. She had a job. They had lives that didn't mesh together. Permitting herself to dream otherwise would only make it harder. Besides, he'd hurt her once, and he would do it again if she let him. Perhaps he simply meant he wouldn't leave without telling her.

She still didn't even know why he'd left her the first time.

She needed to pull herself together and not let this get all nostalgic. It was sex. *Sex*, she shouted into her head.

But she knew she was lying, to herself and to him. If they stood any chance of hashing things out between them, she needed to open herself up a bit. She took a deep breath. "I don't do casual sex, Mike."

He stared into her eyes, his brows furrowed. "Are you saying you regret what we just did, you don't want to do it again, or it wasn't casual for you?"

"The last one." She swallowed. "I'd be lying if I didn't admit it meant something to me."

He set his forehead against hers again. "I know that, baby."

She wiped the corners of her eyes as he eased her into his arms, turned off the light once more, and dragged her into the same position they'd been in before.

It felt so right.

But she could not trust this feeling to last.

Chapter Eight

MIKE HELD HER sweet body against his. He was still in a state of shock. She hadn't slept with any other man?

Why why why why why did she send him that email telling him she'd moved on? If he meant that much to her, why didn't she fight for him? For them?

Because you didn't contact her, asshole. Not one time. You shook her very foundation with your silence. You destroyed her faith.

He felt like a total dick. As well he should.

She remained awake for a long time, though neither of them spoke. Finally, her breathing evened out and her body relaxed into his embrace. If he had his way, they would stay intertwined forever. Until they died of starvation or something.

He didn't ever want to let her go.

But he also needed to shake some sense into himself. Terrorists were after her. They were also after her father. He needed to come up with a plan and get them on the road tomorrow.

They needed clothes.

They were going to look strange walking into a department store in the morning dressed in last night's rumpled mess. But no way was he going to leave her anywhere to go do the task himself.

They might look like they were taking a simultaneous walk of shame buying clothes together, but it couldn't be avoided.

He breathed in her scent. Damn, he had missed her. What would she say if she found out he had pined for her for twelve years? Granted, he hadn't been nearly as saintly about it. He'd slept with other women. He'd had several short relationships.

But he hadn't come close to making a commitment to another human being for the same reasons she'd listed. No one lit a spark like she had. It didn't matter that they'd been so young. He had loved her. He'd known it then, and he'd never doubted it.

Could he dare to hope he could have her now?

No. Not a chance. He was playing with fire.

It didn't matter how well they connected. How deep into her eyes he looked. How great the sex was. He'd betrayed her. She would not be able to forgive him, and he was a dick for fucking her even now without showing her all the cards.

He groaned inwardly.

Every inch of him was wrapped around her, touching as much of her skin as he could. It might have to last him a lifetime.

It took several hours before he fell asleep and it seemed like only moments before he jerked awake.

Something had woken him. A sound.

"Mike, it's your phone." Her voice was scratchy from sleep. Deep. Sexy.

His cock jumped to attention as he squeezed her tight, kissed her shoulder, and then rolled away to grab his phone off the bedside table.

The screen showed Greg Lambert, and a shocking time of eight o'clock. The room was pitch dark behind the curtains.

"Dorsen here," he answered.

"You safe?"

"Yep. We stopped at a hotel in between cities."

"Good. Update: My men didn't make it to the house before the guys took off. Can you get me video of them?"

"Yes. There were cameras, but I think they were smart. Not likely to see much. I'll get them though."

"Okay. What's your plan?"

"Don't have one. We have nothing with us. Need to get supplies."

"Money? Weapons?"

"No. Got that covered. We don't have clothes. Shoes."

"Ah. Okay. I couldn't imagine you ever unprepared." Lambert chuckled.

"I'm a dude. I don't need more than the pack that was with me. But I don't think Zola's going to want to spend days on end in a dress and spike heels." He twisted to grin at her, setting a hand on her belly. She'd rolled to her back and stared up at him, worrying her lip. Unable to stop himself, he pulled the offended lip from her teeth with his thumb.

Now that they were awake, he realized the room wasn't as dark as he thought. Enough light was leaking around the edge of the curtains to cast the room in a soft glow.

"How's Ms. Carver?" Lambert pointedly asked, his tone and the way he drawled out the words indicating he was curious about how close Mike and Zola were.

"She's alive. Pissed. Stressed. Angry."

"Good. Those qualities will keep her from getting killed. You got this?"

"Of course."

"Okay. I'm trying to track down anything we can to find the people hunting her. Gonna assume the guys from last night were hired."

"Undoubtedly."

"You keep low. I'll catch up with you soon."

"On it." Mike ended the call, set the phone back on the end table, and rolled back toward Zola. He tossed one leg over her, straddling her sexy body, and tugged the sheet down so he could see her chest.

She squirmed.

He threaded his fingers with hers and lifted their combined hands over her head, pressing them into the mattress as he leaned forward to kiss her. "Best night of sleep I've ever had."

She grinned. "Me too. I wasn't sure I could relax with you touching me…everywhere, but somehow I felt…safe."

"Good." He kissed her again. And again. They needed to shower, check out, and get on the road. Or maybe he needed to kiss her some more.

She was addictive.

He owned so many of her firsts. She was thirty years old, and he owned her virginity, twice in a way, and from her reaction, he gathered he was the first man to go down on her. He also owned her first night sleeping with a man and possibly her love. No way would he say anything like that out loud. It was too soon. She wouldn't say it either, but she had once loved him. He cringed inwardly, knowing she would never let him have that love again after she found out everything that had transpired all those years ago.

Shit. One day. Two nights. Best sex of his life.

"Where are we going to go?" she asked between his kisses.

"No place particular. I just want to keep us moving. We'll meander north I think. I don't want to be too far away from Connecticut in case something happens, but I do want to keep a safe distance."

She nodded and then inhaled long and slow. "I think I need to speak to my father soon." The way she chewed her lip again told him she thought he might not agree.

He knew this moment was coming. He couldn't keep her all to himself forever. He'd never agreed with her father. And he still probably wouldn't when it came to Zola, but the man was her dad. And Mike intended to respect him. "Of course. Why don't you call him?" He held his breath, knowing full well that a conversation with her dad would change everything.

She nodded, sighing, but she didn't seem ready to jump out of bed and grab the phone.

Somehow he didn't think she meant to speak to Richard about this terrorist situation. She intended to let him know she was with Mike. Perhaps she was concerned her father still wouldn't approve of him.

Or was there more to it? Maybe she hadn't divulged everything about the circumstances surrounding that email. He couldn't blame her. He certainly hadn't been forthcoming about his role.

Mike had a lot to atone for. No way in hell was he going to make things worse by attempting to alienate Zola from her father. It would bite him in the ass in the long run. There was a good chance she would cut off his balls anyway when she found out what he'd done. At the very least, he wanted to take the moral high ground from this moment forward. Even if it destroyed his tenuous relationship with Zola.

After her admission last night about this not being casual for her, it was even more imperative that he tell her what a dick move he'd made that first semester in college.

She interrupted his thinking. "It's early still. I'll call him later."

"My phone is secure. You can call him from it anytime." He released her wrists and propped himself on his side next to her.

She rolled onto her side to face him. "Why? I would think you would be unenthusiastic about me talking to my dad." Her voice was sarcastic. "A man who worked his ass off to keep us from dating. A man who did his best to make sure we split up. That dad?"

He nodded. She only knew the half of it. "He's still

your father. If you want to speak to him, I will never stop you. *Never*." He punctuated that last word with another kiss. "We're adults now. We were kids before. Adults influenced us then. But we make our own choices now. I'm not going to cower to your father. Nor will I avoid him. No matter what happens between us—and I hope to God we can mend our relationship—Richard Carver will still be your father. I will show respect toward him under any circumstances. For you."

She was breathing heavier when he finished speaking. A tear leaked from her eye also.

He leaned down to kiss it away, the salty drop reminding him what an ass he'd been and how many years he'd lost.

And the irony? The shit of the whole thing? He'd lost this perfect woman because he'd had way too much respect for her father. Was it worth it?

He definitely needed to grow some balls and fill her in on some more of the details about the events from that fall twelve years ago. There was a risk that her father might reveal details when she spoke to him, details Mike himself should unveil before then.

On the other hand, it would be difficult to continue to keep her safe if she was pissed. Any number of things could happen. She might even insist on separating herself from Mike, and he wouldn't take that risk. Maybe he was a coward, but her safety was also forefront in his mind.

He needed to tell her, but not now. Later. He could talk when they stopped next. *Chicken.* "Let's shower. Get on the road. Keep moving. We'll stop and pick up supplies."

She shook her head, surprising him. *What now?*

"Let's have sex again. *Then* we can start on that list of yours."

His cock jumped to attention. The one currently bobbing between them half-erect. It switched to fully erect in a heartbeat. Her plan was better.

She shocked him further by setting her palms on his chest and shoving him to his back. As if she were truly controlling the situation, she rose beside him.

He landed hard, laughing. "Feisty."

"Mmm." She scrambled from the bed, yanked the curtains a few inches apart, and bounded back to kneel next to him. "I wanted to see better."

He reached for her.

She batted at his hands. "We've had sex two times and you controlled everything both times." She grabbed his wrist and set it above his head, making his dick even harder. "Let me rephrase. *I've* had sex only twice in my life. Yours is the only…member I've seen. I have never touched it. I haven't tasted it. You owe me."

The laughter that erupted from deep in his belly made her frown.

"What's so funny?"

"Member?" He grasped his erection with the hand she hadn't manipulated and stroked it from the base to the tip. "My dick doesn't really like that term. Cock. Dick. You pick."

She flushed a gorgeous shade of red. "Right. Well, forgive me."

111

He still chuckled. "Always. And I'll let you explore all you want as long as you let me return the favor."

"You've already seen your fill…down there. And, and, tasted too." She shuddered.

He tried not to laugh harder. He truly did.

She swatted at his chest playfully. "Stop it. I'm not used to your crass words."

"Pussy?" he teased. "Your *down there*?"

She pursed her lips, refusing to meet his gaze, and turned her attention to his *member* and then the rest of his body. Her heated stare burned through him. When she perched over his legs, stroked her fingers over his mangled knee, and then leaned forward to kiss the scars above his kneecap, he swallowed hard, his laughter dying immediately.

Next, her small hand wrapped around his cock and stroked it almost imperceptibly. "Tell me what you like," she whispered, completely serious.

God, he adored her. "Baby, if you're touching my cock, you can virtually do no wrong."

"It's smoother than I expected."

"Mmm." It was going to be tough keeping up a running commentary about his junk with her stroking it.

She ran her finger through the slit, spreading his precome. And then he nearly died when she lifted it to her lips and sucked it clean. "Salty," she announced.

His eyes were wide, but he couldn't speak.

She resumed her inspection, teasing him mercilessly while he mostly held his breath to avoid shooting his load prematurely.

When she reached lower to cup his balls, he flinched.

She yanked her hand away. "Sorry. Not there?"

He grabbed her wrist and set her hand back on his nuts. "Oh, baby. Definitely there. Just be gentle. You can hold my cock fairly tight, but my balls are sensitive. Your touch draws them inward. I'm going to come if you do this much longer." He let go of her wrist and flattened his palm on the bed. His other hand above his head curled into a fist in the sheet.

She resumed.

He watched. Best show of his life. And another first gifted to him from Zola. She stopped his breath with her raw beauty. Her hair hung in messy curls around her face, the strawberry-blond creating a halo from the shaft of light behind her.

Her tits swayed next to him. He longed to hold them, clasp them, weigh them, suckle them… So many plans. But not now. Now was her turn. He wouldn't deny her this.

Even if it killed him.

And it almost did when she leaned forward and licked the tip of his cock. She held the shaft in her hand, her fingers not quite reaching all the way around, and she guided him to her mouth.

His heart skipped a beat just watching. It was hard to focus, but he didn't want to miss a moment of her blossoming.

She didn't look to him for confirmation before she boldly sucked him into her mouth.

He held very still. *Do not come. Do not come.* He forced himself to think of anything not sexy while she let him slide deeper between her lips. Road kill. Cockroaches on the counter. Mosquitoes nipping at him.

Nothing worked.

He groaned into the silence.

She didn't remove him from her mouth, but she did lift her gaze and her eyelids in question.

He released the sheet above his head and let his hand fly forward to grasp her thigh. "That's so good, baby. Perfect." He wasn't humoring her. She truly could do no wrong.

She sucked harder. Deeper. When her little tongue dragged up the side of his shaft, he bit his tongue. When her cheeks hollowed as she sucked him back in deeper, he squeezed her thigh. He cupped the back of her head with his other hand, not pushing her, but encouraging her.

When he knew he couldn't keep from coming another moment, he squeezed her neck. "You gotta stop, baby. I'm gonna come."

Instead of heeding his advice, she flicked her tongue through the slit at the top and then sucked him faster.

He lost control, his hands no longer gripping her. Instead, they loosened but wouldn't accept commands from his brain. He closed his eyes, bucked toward her mouth, and moaned loudly as his come shot into her.

Damn it if she didn't swallow him also.

He pulsed for longer than ever, copious amounts of his come hitting the back of her throat. And his gorgeous, sexy, vixen swallowed every drop.

When she finally lifted off, she licked her lips and smiled. "I did that to you," she declared triumphantly.

He released a chuckle. "You definitely did." It took several moments for him to regain full control of his arms and legs, and then he lurched forward and flipped her onto her back.

She giggled. The sound was musical. She hadn't laughed much in the two days they'd been together. The tone vibrated through the air, reminding him of years ago. She'd laughed a lot back then. He'd lived for that sound. It had kept him going during any dark moment.

And here she was. Not an apparition but the real deal. His again. In his arms. In his bed. Her mouth still slick from his come.

God, he wanted her. He'd just come hard, and already he was stiff again.

Suddenly, a new realization jolted Mike so hard he flinched. This woman, the love of his life, wasn't some sweet, innocent girl out of a desire to remain celibate. It wasn't an act she put on because she was too much of a goody two shoes to sleep around. It was him. He was it for her.

She hadn't saved herself from men because she was a prude. On the contrary, she was eager and willing and even demanding in bed. She'd saved herself because she wanted to be those things with Mike.

Damn. If he'd been standing, he would have sunk to his knees. How would he ever be worthy of her devotion?

At the moment, he needed to worship her body the way she deserved. The way he'd always dreamed of.

He wanted her to experience everything. He wanted her to feel the same loss of control she'd just given him.

He wanted everything.

Chapter Nine

THE WIND KNOCKED out of her as she landed on her back.

The intense look on his face made her shudder. He would never know how much it meant to her that he'd let her do that without interruption. Sure, he teased her at the beginning, but not in a malicious way.

Now he stared down at her like she was a feast he intended to devour. And she was already aroused just from swallowing his…cock.

Her sex—pussy—was wet. She felt restless. She reached for him, needing contact. A kiss. His hands. Anything.

He shook his head, continuing to gaze at her body as if he needed to memorize it. He reached tentatively with shaky fingers to stroke them up her arm and then down between her breasts. He danced the tips over her stomach until it hallowed.

He smiled, not looking at her face but watching her reaction to his touch. Without warning, he lifted his fingers to graze over her nipple. First one and then the other.

She arched her chest upward, squeezing her lips together to keep from moaning and breaking the spell.

When he lightly pinched her swollen bud, she let out a sharp squeal and grabbed his wrist. It hadn't hurt. It simply shocked her.

Wetness pooled between her legs.

Without a word, he grabbed her wrist with his free hand and hauled it over her head. Much the same as she'd done to him. He pressed her palm into the mattress and released, a silent command to leave her hand there. Her other arm was trapped at her side between her hip and his knees.

He teased her nipple again, pinching it harder, twisting it slightly, and then tugging.

So many sensations. So much pleasure. She was overloaded. She couldn't find the words to speak. And what would she say? Stop? More?

For long minutes he switched back and forth, tormenting her nipples until she thought she might come. She began to squirm.

"Spread your legs, baby." His voice was hoarse. Ragged.

She separated her knees.

"Wider, Zola. Let me get between them." He lifted one knee to set it between hers and then waited for her to comply so he could set his other in between her thighs also.

He'd been in that position last night. He'd been there the first time they had sex also. But this...this was more. There was no rush. No demanding need to...fuck. He had all the time in the world. And he obviously intended to take advantage of it.

He pressed her thighs farther apart and then set his hands flat on her legs at the apex and pulled her labia apart with his thumbs.

She'd never felt so exposed. The wetness gathered at her entrance was embarrassing. Perhaps that was irrational, but she couldn't help it.

"So pink. Swollen. Sexy. Ready. For me."

His words made her hotter. His stare brought unimaginable arousal to the surface. And she wanted more. She wanted everything. She wanted to feel this tight ball of need for as long as she could. If he made her wait, she would endure it, because it was so precious. That edge. That feeling of need so intense it almost shattered. Almost. But not quite.

"Love the noises you make, baby."

She was making a noise? How was that possible with her lips pursed shut? A low hum vibrated through her. Wow.

He flicked his gaze to hers, slowly smiled, and then resumed his study of her pussy. When he pulled the hood back from her clit, she shivered.

He set a hand on her lower belly inches above her clit to hold her steady. With his other hand, he dragged a finger through her wetness and circled her nub.

It wasn't enough. And it was too much. Could someone actually die from sensation overload?

Her head lolled to the side and she gasped for air as if there wasn't enough oxygen in the room. How did he manage to drive her so insane with not much more than his gaze and the slightest touch of his fingers in all the wrong places?

Perhaps she was a fool for holding back all these years when she could have been enjoying sex like this with any number of men. Right?

She knew the answer to that was *no*. It wasn't about just sex. It had to be with the right person for it to feel like this. Like the Earth stopped spinning and waited for her to experience total nirvana.

Only Mike could bring this out of her.

Only Mike…

He reached inside her with one finger, making her mouth open wider. She wanted to scream or say something, but no sound came out.

And then her entire body electrified when he spun his hand around and dragged that finger back out of her, crossing over some elusive spot that did indeed stop time.

Holy mother of God. What the…

Again. And again.

She drew her knees up, grasping his thighs. He had to stop. Whatever he was doing, he had to stop. It was too much. She was losing control. She grabbed his wrist with both hands. "Mike…"

He used his other hand to tug her free, one fist at a time. "Baby, let it go. Just feel. Don't try to stop it." He did it again, adding another finger. Some spot inside her made her head spin. Her G-spot? Was that a real thing?

She panted.

He thrust faster, his palm slapping into her clit with every pass.

She gasped, grabbing the sheets at her sides to hold on

to something tangible while the world spun off its axis. She arched her chest upward, her knees grasping his thighs, her heels digging into the mattress, her head tipped back. She'd never felt so totally out of control. Bliss was a breath away. She could feel it.

It scared her. To death.

Too much sensation. She felt exposed. Raw. Like her skin had disappeared and he could see inside her.

And she would give this to him. Because she couldn't not.

He fucked her with those fingers, adding a third. "That's it, baby. Let it go. Give it to me." He held her torso firmly to the bed, and he watched her unravel.

And she let go. She screamed as the most powerful orgasm burst free. She gripped the bedding tighter, squeezed his thighs so hard it hurt, and she cried out her release. Fluid rushed from her pussy to coat his hand. God, she hoped it was normal.

He slowed his movements gradually as she came down from heaven.

She licked her lips, lowered her chin, and met his gaze.

He released her belly to cup her face, his other hand still moving languidly inside her. "Zola…"

She flushed. He'd watched her come completely un-done.

"Such a gift. I'm humbled."

"Was that? Do women?" she stammered.

He smiled. "Totally normal. Yes. But not all women can do that. Most can't let themselves relax enough to give it up. It takes incredible trust. And Jesus, you have no experience. And…I'm just so very humbled, baby. Thank you."

"Thank *me*?" She squirmed. "Shouldn't I thank *you*?"

He smiled wider. "My pleasure."

Suddenly she knew something with incredible certainty. She needed him inside her. The fullness of his cock filling her. It didn't matter that she'd come hard. She needed him to fill her completely.

She pulled his hand from her pussy and reached for his cock. "Fuck me." The word was unnatural coming off her tongue, but she didn't care. She spread her legs wider, wiggling down the mattress to get better contact. Closer. "Mike, fuck me. Now. Hard."

He tipped his head to one side. "Baby, you have to be sore. And—"

She almost cried or screamed in frustration. "*Mike*," she shouted. "Stop fucking arguing with me. I want you inside me now."

He fell forward, landing on his elbows at her sides. Immediately he thrust into her on a moan. "Zola…"

"God, yes." She grabbed at his back, her fingers digging into him. She wrapped her legs around his waist and held him tight, only giving him enough space to pull out a few inches and slam back in. "Don't be careful with me. Please. Mike. Harder. I need you."

He gave her what she wanted, his lips slamming on hers to devour her while he thrust in and out. She climbed to the top again fast, her body needing another release. It didn't matter that she'd just had her first deep internal orgasm. She wanted more. Insatiable. A driving need.

He fucked her. Just as she imagined it would be. Rough. Fast. Hard.

Yes.

Soft and gentle was good. It was amazing. But now she wanted to experience something else. And he gave it to her.

When she couldn't keep her eyes open any longer, she went into her head, visions of him hovering over her filling her mind's eye to match the reality. And then she was coming again, her pussy grasping at his cock.

And Mike followed her, groaning around his release, still pumping hard, slamming his cock deep, the base hitting her clit with every movement.

When he was spent, he set his forehead on the mattress next to her, gasping for oxygen just as she was. She smoothed her hands up his back and threaded her fingers in his thick hair.

Suddenly, prematurely, he bolted upright, sitting over her, jerking his cock from her. "Shit. Condom."

"Relax," she soothed. "Birth control."

His shoulders slumped as he searched her face. "Thank fuck." He took a deep breath and ran a hand over his head. And then he jerked his gaze to hers again. "Why?"

"Why what?"

"Why the hell are you taking birth control?"

She smirked. "Don't get your panties in a wad, big guy." She grabbed his thighs and rubbed her palms over his skin. "I'm not a liar. Lots of women take birth control these days. Regulate. Cramps. Headaches. The list is long. Welcome to the twenty-first century."

He breathed out a long sigh. "Of course. Sorry. Didn't

mean to accuse you. That came out wrong." He glanced at the spot where his cock was still nestled against her opening. "And I've never once in my life had unprotected sex. Swear. I'm clean."

"Okay." She rubbed his legs again. "I trust you."

"But, now that I have, and with you…" He leaned forward, his hands at the sides of her face. "Gotta say, babe, that was fucking incredible. I'm not going to want to roll another condom on my cock again in this lifetime if I can help it."

She swallowed around his mention of a lifetime, as if he thought they could stay together. She wasn't anywhere near ready to face that possibility. Too many unanswered questions. Too many holes. Too much history.

He ignored her lack of response. "You're so perfect." He gazed down at her until she squirmed under his stare.

"We should get going before they bang on the door and kick us out."

"Yeah." He didn't move.

"Mike?"

"Give me a second."

"'Kay." She felt his intensity in every part of her body.

"I'm sorry."

"For what?" She was confused.

"For ever letting you go."

She nodded. "Why did you?"

He stared at her, his gaze roaming over her body before he said, "It won't happen again."

"Okay." She wasn't sure she could trust him yet. Not with her future. The sex was fantastic. No denying that.

But relationships were based on way more than sex.

"We should go," he stated.

"I mentioned that." She smiled again. "You'll need to get off me."

"Yeah…" He lifted one hand and traced it across her forehead and around her face. And then he touched her lips. He drew the bottom one down.

She stuck her tongue out far enough to lick the pad of his finger.

Seconds ticked by again. Did he need to say something else?

If he did, he reined it back in, finally rolling off her to collapse next to her on his back. "Who's going to get up first?" he asked, out of breath.

"Mmm. The shower might be big enough for two."

Chapter Ten

MIKE HELD HER hand tight as they entered the closest department store. Too tight. His demeanor had totally switched to serious work mode the moment they left the hotel room. He was all business. And he was stressed.

Was she in any more danger than yesterday? She didn't think so. She suspected his mood was due to how he felt about her today.

Not that he hadn't made it clear he adored her yesterday, but something between them had shifted, and now nothing would ever be the same.

She felt it too. A change in the air.

She felt freer, while at the same time no longer her own person. They were connected in a way that bound them together without papers or permission or judges or ministers. They had forged a bond that joined them on its own. And it scared her to death. She wasn't sure she was ready for anything as serious as what was unspoken between them, especially since there were still unanswered questions between them. Mike was holding something back, something important, something about why he'd let her go all those years ago.

Should she pressure him into telling her? So far, he'd seemed reluctant. Or hesitant. Or...scared. To be honest, she was a bit afraid to hear his answer too. Maybe that was what kept her from pressing the issue.

They were moving through the store at warp speed.

"Mike." She tried to get his attention, tugging on her hand.

He glanced down at her. "What?"

"You're going too fast. I can't keep up. We're safe. No one's following us. Slow down. I need you to let me go so I can grab some clothes." She wanted a little privacy. No matter how much had transpired between them in the last twelve hours, she didn't enjoy the idea of him watching her pick out panties, bras, and whatever other personal items she might grab.

"Not going to let you go, Zola." He slowed his pace, but he still directed them toward the women's department. "I want to get this done." He glanced at her and then looked around.

Suddenly she realized he wasn't simply worked up over the terrorist threat; he was jealous about other people seeing her in this dress. She jerked her hand free and narrowed her gaze when he spun around. "Stop."

"Stop what?" He closed the distance between them until they were standing so close she had to glance back and forth to see both his eyes.

"Mike. I'm not naked. Yes, it's not exactly what most people wear first thing in the morning to go shopping, but

I'm covered. Get a grip. Let me shop. Go get what you need."

He shook his head and leaned down to take her lips in a quick kiss, his hand snaking around to her back. Heck, she even had a coat on. No one would ever know her back was bare under the thick layer of warmth.

Her shoulders sagged as she determined she wasn't going to win this battle. "Fine. Follow me. I'll get what I need. And then I'll go with you."

"That was the plan." At least he broke a half smile.

She rolled her eyes and led them deeper into the clothing section. She quickly grabbed jeans in her size, two shirts, and then decided to get a long sweater and a pair of leggings.

He lifted a brow, but didn't say a word.

She headed for lingerie next, her hands shaking as she chose panties and a bra. She'd never bought anything incredibly sexy before. And she didn't intend to start now. Silk. Lace. Functional. When she finished, she glanced up at him to suggest they move to the shoe department.

But his face made her change her mind. She blew out a long breath at the tight frown he held, dropped all four pairs of panties and the bra in the nearest bin, and started over.

What the hell was she doing? It took determination to make her way to a far sexier section where she picked out two skimpy bikini briefs and two thongs. The bra she grabbed had less material than lace and she prayed it would support her.

Mike looked far more pleased, and it unnerved her how

he'd manipulated the entire thing without a word.

She scowled and marched them to the men's section.

Fifteen minutes later, they were back in the SUV.

Zola was still laughing at the look on the clerk's face when she told the woman she was going to change in the fitting room after the purchase.

Good thing the fitting rooms were for both sexes because the closest Mike was willing to go with permitting this plan was to stand outside hers while she changed and then swapping places. He took less than fifteen seconds and looked a bit pale and panicked when he opened the door.

His idea had been for them to get naked in the car. *Right…*

Back on the road, she pleaded with him to stop for coffee and won. Not that it was difficult.

"We had two cups before we left the hotel."

"And I want another one," she argued.

He turned left at the next light, and five minutes later, she was sipping a third cup of coffee and munching on a muffin.

"Have you spoken to your father?" he asked.

She lifted a brow, licking a crumb from her lip. "When would I have done that without your knowledge? I haven't even gone to the bathroom alone."

He shot her a glance. "That's an exaggeration. I left you in the bathroom before we checked out."

"Uh-huh. After washing me with your own hands and then drying me off."

"Hey," he shot back. "The idea to shower at the same time was yours." He grabbed her hand and held it in his lap. "I was just trying to speed up the process while I had the bar of soap already in my hands." At least he lost the ability to continue to look so severe and started chuckling. For a moment she was worried he was dead serious.

"And the shampoo?" she teased.

"I squirted too much in my palm. No sense wasting it."

She giggled silently and hid her expression behind her cup of coffee.

Mike's phone rang, making her flinch.

He let go of her hand to connect the Bluetooth. "Dorsen speaking."

"Mike."

"Hey. Anything new to report?"

"Yeah. Ditch the car."

"Fuck."

"Yep. Do it now."

"On it." He disconnected, hit the gas, and sped off at the next exit.

Zola stiffened and set her nearly empty cup in a cup holder. She held on to the dash with one hand and the door with her other. The car? How was the car compromised? "What are you going to do?"

"Not sure yet. Thinking."

She left him alone. It may have been twelve years since she spent any time with him, but assuming he hadn't had a total personality switch, he needed her to be quiet so he could concentrate. He'd been that way every time they studied. He wasn't the watch-TV-while-eating-a-snack-while-making-out-with-his-girlfriend sort of studier.

And apparently that hadn't changed.

He tapped the steering wheel rapidly with his fingers while he turned several times. Finally, he pulled into a busy section of whatever town they were in and scanned the entire area, dipping his head to see better. His gaze shot back and forth multiple times until he sat upright and pulled into a small parking garage.

He circled the bottom floor and continued upward until they were somewhere near the top. Slowing to a crawl, he eased down the aisles until he finally pulled into a spot between an extended van and a wall.

"What's the plan?" she asked confused.

"We leave this car here. Take our belongings, and go find a new one."

Right. That sounded so simple. Except *not*.

Mike grabbed their shopping bags and his backpack as Zola rounded the car. She tried to take something from him, but he shifted the bags to one hand and took her hand with his free one without a word. "Let's go."

She was glad for the comfortable clothes because she had to walk fast to keep up with his pace.

His brow remained furrowed while they made their way down the stairs and out of the garage.

When they stepped into the light of day, cool air hit her in the face. She gathered her coat tighter around her and leaned closer to Mike in attempt to calm him. It didn't work. He was still stiff.

"Where are we?"

"Suffolk. And thank goodness because it will be easy to rent a car here."

"What are you going to do about the rental car? The

one we just left I mean."

"Someone will come pick it up and handle it later."

She decided to stop asking questions and let him concentrate. Luckily they rounded a corner to a populated area, and Mike flagged down a taxi. Ten minutes later they were at the counter asking for a rental car.

Zola let Mike handle things, keeping her mouth shut, and doing no more than lifting an eyebrow when he pulled out an ID, credit card, and insurance with another identity. She didn't change her face, comment, question, or break a smile until they were inside the newer car buckling their seat belts. "You just happen to have another identity on you?" She laughed as they pulled out of the spot.

Mike finally smiled too. "Always."

"And you also carry a lot of cash I noticed."

He glanced at her as he turned onto the main street. "I didn't take on the job of protecting you unprepared."

"Now I see why you carry that pack around. What else is in that bag of yours?"

"You've seen most of it. I never travel without cash, weapons, and identification."

"You think whoever is tracking us can trace us through the rental car or credit cards." It wasn't a question. She shuddered at the realization that someone had already.

"I know they can." He entered the highway, his gaze darting all around. And then he set a hand on hers and squeezed. "Don't worry. We're not being followed, and no one has any information about the identity I just used."

She nodded, still feeling nervous, but beginning to realize Mike could and would keep her safe at all costs. Not just because of how he felt about her, but because he was that good at his job. Rocking that boat right now was not a good idea.

She needed to call her father. If he heard about this, he would be worried. But calling him while Mike was white-knuckling the steering wheel in fear for her life was also a bad idea. Not now. Later.

She wasn't sure if her dad even realized who was keeping her safe. What would he say when he found out it was Mike Dorsen? She wasn't in the mood to deal with the hassle of facing the inquisition yet. She hadn't been in the mood for two days. How long could she hide?

Half of her feared her dad still wouldn't approve of Mike, and she was too tired to deal with what that would mean to her right now. She would have to put her foot down and tell him to back off. Her relationships, with Mike or anyone, were none of his business. He needed to understand that the reason she'd shut herself off from men altogether was because the best one she'd ever met had slipped through her fingers.

According to Richard Carver, Mike had never been good enough for her. He hadn't come from money. He didn't have parents. He wasn't from the right side of the tracks. Never mind he was a good person who had everything going for him and managed to get through school and go on to become a Navy SEAL.

Maybe she should be pissed to hell that he'd had a hand in helping break up her relationship, but in the end, it had been Zola herself who sent that final detrimental email to Mike. She'd taken her father's advice, yes, but he didn't type the words. She did.

Perhaps she'd ruined the best thing that had ever happened to her, and she had to live with that. But at the time, it had seemed logical. After all, Mike hadn't answered *any* email she sent. She'd been worried and angry and hurt and stressed, and the reality was that if she had it to do over again, she might take her father up on the same advice.

No. She couldn't blame her father. But she sure didn't want to make that call to tell him Mike was back in her life and she hoped it could be more than a fling.

It would help if Mike would provide her with more information about his role in their breakup. Why had he ghosted her? And why did he accept her lie without a fight? So many questions, none of which had anything to do with the advice her father gave her.

Would her father see him differently now? Or would it still matter that Mike didn't have a prestigious family background suitable for Richard Carver's daughter?

Mike took her hand again and squeezed it between them. "You want to use my phone while we drive?" Could he read her mind?

She squeezed his fingers back. "No. Not in the car. I'll do it later, when we stop." *Do you want to fill in some of the holes in our story before I call my dad?* She closed her eyes, leaning her head back against the headrest, unable to verbalize that question. Maybe a part of her didn't want to hear the answer. She racked her brain trying to think what he was holding back. Had he found someone else as soon as he'd moved to Berkeley and moved on that fast?

This entire thing was absurd. She'd been with Mike

two nights. Not even forty-eight hours, and already she felt drawn to him. Like no time had passed, in a way. Though that wasn't the point.

Her mind wandered back to her father.

It didn't really matter whether or not things with Mike worked out in the long run. What mattered was that it was her choice. Her life.

Why was she dragging her feet?

If Richard Carver couldn't accept that his daughter had every right to enter into a relationship with anyone she pleased, then she needed to know that. She was a grown woman who would make her own choices, and no way in hell was she going to permit his interference at the age of thirty.

After putting her thoughts aside, she focused on Mike. "Tell me everything about yourself. Everything you've done for twelve years."

He flashed her a smile. "We covered most of it."

She shook her head. "Not even close. I want to know you better."

And so began a long aimless drive north that ended with Zola so enamored with the man next to her, it was indeed like no time had passed between them. Most of that time, he held her hand against his thigh or sometimes rubbed it across his cheek. She wasn't sure he was even aware of the intimacy.

They took turns asking questions and listening. They discussed everything that had happened between their breakup and now, though she intentionally avoided asking him any more questions about why he'd ended their relationship. Not in the car. Not while he was driving. When would it seem appropriate to insist he talk about it?

They also went back over the case files for the three people she had helped convict in the last several years. Though the paperwork had been left behind and they didn't have a computer, she knew every detail and learned he had an incredible memory also.

Mike touched base several times during the day with his contact at the CIA, updating him often of their whereabouts. As they approached the outskirts of a small town, she grew silent, staring out the window and pondering what she wanted to say to her father. She couldn't stall any longer. As soon as they got a hotel room, she would need to call him.

It was late afternoon when Mike pulled into a spot outside a moderately priced hotel and got them a room. She had been concentrating on touching base with her father for a while without saying much to Mike. Perhaps she was overthinking things and he wouldn't even remember Mike that well. But Zola didn't believe that. She felt confident her father would not be pleased to find out she was with Mike. Not just with Mike, but *with* Mike.

He must have read her mind again because as soon as they were settled in the room, he handed her his phone. "Call him."

She nodded, her fingers shaking as she took the cell.

"I'll wait in the hallway so you'll have some privacy," Mike said, turning toward the door.

"No. Stay. This affects you too. There can't be more secrets between us." She stared at him, wondering if he might want to clear up any secrets before she made the call.

He lowered himself into the room's only chair instead while she settled on the edge of the bed and dialed.

"Hello?" her father answered on the first ring.

"Dad, it's me."

"Zola. Thank God. I've been worried. They told me you're in good hands and safe, but I worried anyway."

She didn't want to waste time beating around the bush. "I'm with Mike Dorsen."

He sucked in a quick breath. "Dorsen? How?"

She felt a certain level of snarkiness creep up her spine. "Contrary to your beliefs about Mike when I was in high school, he actually made something of himself. He was with the Navy SEALs for a while in fact. And the government contracted him to keep me alive." She knew these first words were antagonistic, but she didn't care.

Her father sighed. "I see. Are you okay? Are you safe?"

"I'm sure I'll be safe no matter where I am as long as Mike is with me. He's quite capable of protecting me." Her voice was higher than usual, and she knew she wasn't hiding her stress. She stared at the floor to keep from watching Mike's expression.

Her father drew in a slow breath. "You sound pissed. I suppose he told you about the money. Why are you so mad at *me*? I would think you'd be at least as angry with him."

Money? Zola felt like she'd been punched in the gut. She didn't move or breathe. The blood drained from her face.

So this was the secret Mike had been holding back. Her father paid him to stay away from her? What the fuck? She started shaking.

It all fell into place. The emails. The lack of answers. Mike had taken blackmail money from her own father in exchange for leaving her alone.

Her father couldn't see her reaction and he continued to speak, rambling about the money he'd sent Mike and how he thought it would help Mike get through school and get a head start in life. His words started to blur in her mind. What the hell was going on? Her face heated. She felt faint. She couldn't lift her gaze to look at Mike. Her head was tipped toward the floor and heavy.

Still he kept speaking. "I wanted you to feel like you had the upper hand by sending him that email telling him you had moved on and found someone else. It was wrong of me to interfere. Please forgive me. If you can forgive Mike, surely you can forgive me too. I'm your father. You're my only daughter. And I love you more than my own life."

Her brain scrambled as his words tossed around in her head, making no sense. She had no intention of telling her father this was the first she'd heard of any money. That was between her and Mike.

Her boyfriend took a payoff from her father? And he didn't tell her?

Her heart beat wildly, and she didn't want to give either of them the satisfaction of knowing what she felt. She had made this call to let her father know Mike was back in her life. She'd dragged her feet like a baby because she hadn't wanted to face her father's reaction. She'd worried her father would think she was foolish to let Mike back in after the way he'd summarily dropped her all those years ago. And all the while, she'd been worrying about the wrong things.

Her father obviously assumed Mike had told her about the money.

And Mike? He'd let her make this call without telling her he'd taken money to break up with her. He'd known this might happen.

She wanted to slap him. She wanted to scream. How could he do this to her? She couldn't face him. Or her dad. Instead, she managed to find the strength to push herself off the bed and mutter a goodbye, not caring that she was cutting her father off mid-conversation. And then she strode into the bathroom and shut the door silently behind her without glancing at Mike.

She had no choice but to stay in the hotel with him. He was her protection for the near future. Perhaps she could request someone else tomorrow, but it was late tonight. For the time being she needed to pull herself together and think.

Chapter Eleven

M IKE'S HEART STOPPED beating as the only woman
he'd ever loved walked out of the room. He'd been
at war with himself all day over the decision not to tell her
about the check.

Part of him had hoped Richard wouldn't mention that
detail yet, though in the long run the truth would have
come out. Eventually Mike would have told her himself.
The tenuous thin string holding Zola to him for the last
few days eventually had to break. There was no way to
avoid it.

Perhaps it was inexcusable of him to allow her to fall
for him all over again without telling her about that fucking
check. He'd acted cowardly for two reasons. One, he'd
been desperate to reconnect with her if only for a few days.
And two, he was afraid about her safety as soon as this cat
was out of the bag. His greatest fear was that she would tell
him to go to hell, leaving her without the protection he
truly didn't want to entrust to someone else.

He'd known the instant her father mentioned the money without hearing a word of his end of the conversation. She had stiffened and frozen. He'd wanted to go to her but had forced himself to remain in his seat. He would have to face the music. He allowed this train to derail all by himself, and he deserved everything Zola dished out.

Except that was not how it went down.

His heart pounded. She'd left the room so abruptly without saying a word. The last thing he expected was for her to shut down and calmly leave the room. It would have been better if she screamed at him, threw things, demanded an explanation. This silence was far more difficult to endure.

He would give this to her. She deserved some time to process before he tried to explain himself. For what it was worth. He reminded himself that no matter what happened between him and Zola, he needed to keep her safe. That was his top priority.

He closed his eyes for a few seconds and took a deep breath. *You deserve this. Keep her safe.* The shower came on.

He needed to think. Stay alert in the face of this new crisis.

As he opened his phone to call Lambert, he hefted the backpack onto the bed and unzipped it.

It was time to let Lambert in on the saga.

"Dorsen. What's the latest?"

"We stopped at a hotel for the night. Zola just spoke to her father."

"Good. She used the secure phone?"

"Yes. But, Greg, there's something you need to know."

"What?" His voice sounded higher in pitch.

"I know Zola."

"What are you talking about? What do you mean you *know* her?"

"I guess I should say, I knew her. In high school. We dated."

"Fuck." Lambert's voice rose. "And you didn't think to tell me this before?"

"I thought it. I intentionally didn't do it."

"Fuck," he repeated. "You telling me you're too invested to keep this woman safe?"

"No. I'm telling you I knew her. She'll be safe with me." He spoke in a deeper voice, enunciating his words, making it clear he would not be removed from this job.

Lambert groaned. "Don't make me regret this. It will be super fucking messy if this goes bad. For the entire country."

"I'm clear on that. We're holed up for the night in an out-of-the-way hotel. Safe."

Lambert sighed heavily. "Call me in the morning so I know you're still not dead."

"Of course." He ended the call, tossed the phone on the bed, and opened the backpack.

ZOLA WAS FURIOUS. She needed to calm down and think.

She stood under the hot water for so long her fingers were wrinkly. When she finally flipped it off and grabbed a towel, she was exhausted. Her adrenaline rush was gone, leaving her depleted, but no less angry.

Her dad had sent Mike money to pay him to leave her

alone? That was unimaginable. But far more unimaginable was Mike accepting the cash and doing her father's bidding.

She was pissed as fuck at the situation, but the emotion she felt for Mike after further reflection was sadness. He'd let her down. He'd taken a bribe from her own father. She'd thought he loved her. What stung the most was finding out that there existed a dollar amount that would be enough to give her up. At eighteen she wouldn't have believed that any amount of money in the world would have turned Mike away from her. Apparently she was wrong.

Tears ran down her face. She couldn't stop them, and she was grateful for the noise of the fan in the ceiling that blocked any sounds she couldn't stifle. How much money had he accepted in exchange for walking away from her? It didn't matter. Did she really want to know what she was worth? Even ten million dollars was not enough.

She took a deep breath and tried to pull herself together as she combed through her tangled curls. Her face was red and splotchy. Not a shocker. She splashed cold water on her cheeks and applied some moisturizer.

There was no way to hide her emotions or the fact that she'd been crying. And why bother? The man on the other side of the door had taken money as a bribe from her father to stop seeing her. She wasn't sure who to kill first. The weight of the situation left her feeling very lonely.

She couldn't stay in the bathroom forever though. She also needed clothes. Tucking the towel tight around her, she opened the door.

Mike was sitting on the one and only bed in the room,

his phone in his hand. He was typing rapidly, probably using it as a computer. He lifted his gaze, his face tight with stress.

She shot him a glance and turned around to grab clean clothes from their meager possessions. Why hadn't she bought anything to sleep in that morning? Dammit. She grabbed a pair of panties she wished were more modest now and pondered her options.

"Take one of my T-shirts. It'll be long enough to cover you," he whispered as if he were afraid to speak to her.

His idea wasn't bad though, so she tore into a package of tees and grabbed one.

"Can we talk?"

She shook her head, her back to him. "Not yet."

He sighed. "Okay. If you're done in the bathroom, I'll shower now. Zola…please don't open the door for any reason. I know you're pissed at me. And I understand. But I don't want you to risk your safety."

She kept her back to him, her bottom lip between her teeth while he shuffled across the floor and entered the bathroom. As soon as the door snicked shut, she dropped the towel and hurried to cover herself with the T-shirt and then panties. The tee was white and revealing even though it hung below her ass. The panties were way too sexy, and he'd been with her when she bought them.

She climbed onto the bed, shoving the backpack he'd left there out of the way. Crossing her legs in front of her, she stared at the bag and allowed curiosity to get the better of her. What did he carry around in there?

She knew the basics, but how many weapons did he

have and how much cash?

The zipper was open, a few papers sticking out. She lifted the front flap and slowly reached forward to pick up a gun with her tentative fingers. Was it loaded? She set it down next to her and opened the bag wider. There was another gun deeper in the bottom. She ignored that one to grab the envelope on top. It was filled with cash. Lots of cash.

Jesus. Tens. Twenties. Hundreds. No wonder he had no trouble paying in cash everywhere they went. If she didn't know better, she would guess he was a bank robber or a drug dealer.

Another pile of paper caught her eye. A bundle of tri-folded pages with a rubber band around it. She grabbed that next. Curious. Not giving a fuck about his privacy.

The moment she tugged off the rubber band and opened the top page, she stopped breathing. These were the emails she sent him the month they went away to college. He'd printed them…

She glanced at the bathroom door. The shower was running. Did she risk looking at the pages to remind herself of her words?

Who the fuck cared? So what if he caught her? They were *her* emails.

He kept them…

What did that even mean?

The man traveled around with only the most important items in his world at his fingertips, and among those items were five printed emails written from a high school sweetheart? One for whom he took a bribe to break up with by way of a ghosting?

With a deep breath, she faced the paper in her hand. This one was the last one she sent.

She scanned the page, knowing full well what she'd said to him. It hurt to remind herself how she'd lied and told him she was with another man. A student from Yale. Older than her. She'd really embellished the total fabrication to make it believable.

A tear ran down her face as she set the first page aside and picked up the next. The second to last email she wrote him was totally different. Still filled with pleading words that he please write back. Was he okay? Was he mad at her for some reason? Did she have the wrong email address? Had he not gone to Berkeley after all?

So many questions. She'd had no physical address for him at the time. No phone number. His local phone number had been disconnected. He had never contacted her with a new number, not even to tell her the address of his dorm. But she'd easily figured out what his email address had been, and she'd never gotten a mailer daemon.

The third page made her vision blur with tears. Her desperation and sadness over having lost contact with him was evident. She remembered the day she'd sent that one. It had been raining outside. She'd been in her dorm room, her roommate out for the night.

Zola pressed the paper to her chest and fought back the need to sob out loud. So many memories. So painful. It hurt so badly knowing that while she'd been writing those emails, he'd been enjoying the fruits of her father's bribe. Had he already moved on? Had he been dating other women while she pined after him?

She wanted to scream. Her chest hurt so badly. The betrayal was more than she could bear.

Her knee hit the last two trifolded pages, knocking them so that the little pile fell over. Except there weren't two pages left. There were three. No, the one on the bottom was an envelope.

She knew she had sent five emails in all. What was the envelope?

As her fingers betrayed her and reached for it her gut clenched. It was a letter. The return address was her father's. The handwriting was his too.

She fingered it, letting the previous page she'd been clutching fall to the bed.

Oh. My. God. He carries my emails. And a letter from my father? What the fuck alternate universe was she living in?

As she eased the envelope open, she was aware the water was no longer running. But she couldn't stop herself. She didn't care if he caught her. It didn't matter. She wanted to know what her father said to him that was so convincing he let her go for a few dollars.

A trifold of paper slid out of the envelope, and when she unfolded it to read her father's words, something fluttered from the center to fall between her legs. She held the letter to one side to see what had fallen and froze.

It was a check. It lay upside down against her foot, but there was no mistaking the back of a check.

The world spun out of control. Her father hadn't said a word about Mike not depositing it.

The ringing in her ears drowned out all other sounds. A

bomb could have fallen next to the bed, and she would have missed it as she stared at that check.

Finally, she lifted it with two fingers as if it were contaminated or covered with fingerprints she needed to protect. When she flipped it over, she saw that it wasn't a personal check but a cashier's check, and then her eyes bugged out of her head when she saw the dollar amount.

The bathroom door opened, jerking her from her daze. She glanced toward the entrance, tears running down her face. A garbled sob escaped.

Mike met her gaze, his shoulders falling. "Baby…"

She couldn't stop the dam from opening. Wild ugly sobs hitched her breath. Her tears fell as she clutched the unread letter, letting the check land once again on the bed. Her father never would have known if Mike cashed it or not. But nobody in their right mind would receive a cashier's check and hold on to it.

Mike rushed forward, a towel around his waist. "Zola, babe…"

She sucked in oxygen which only fueled her tears. Loud wailing filled the room as if she were in pain.

Mike shoved all the papers away and sat on the edge of the bed. He eased the letter from her grasp and hauled her forward by the shoulders.

She let him, unable to stop him from touching her. Needing the contact. Was it *him* she wanted to hold? Or was it just a warm body in the room needed for comfort from her deep sorrow?

He cupped the back of her head and eased her face against his neck. She didn't wrap her arms around him, but she let him embrace her with his free arm, tucking her against her side awkwardly. He stroked her scalp, his fingers threaded in her hair. "I'm so sorry."

She cried for what seemed like an eternity before she managed to suck in a breath. "You never cashed it." Her voice sounded like it belonged to someone else.

"Of course not."

She lifted her hands to place them on his firm, warm chest and lifted her face to meet his gaze through her blurry vision. "Why didn't you say anything?" She jerked back a few inches so she could see his eyes better. "Why? Dammit, Mike. Why did you break up with me without intending to take the money?"

He swallowed. "What difference does it make that I didn't cash the check? I still let you go. It was the worst decision of my life."

Her eyes widened. "Are you kidding? It makes all the difference in the world." Especially because it was a fuck-ton of money that would have made his life comfortable for years.

Once again, she wanted to slap her father across the face. How dare he?

"He asked me to let you go, babe. I did what he wanted without even consulting you. That's all that matters. It was the wrong choice. I never should've let him manipulate me like that."

Suddenly she needed to know. She needed to read her father's words and know what he said that convinced Mike to let her go. She shoved off his chest and grabbed the paper from her lap.

As she lifted the single sheet of white computer paper, her gaze was already scanning the page.

At first her father pleaded with Mike to give her the space she needed to succeed. He didn't want her to give up her dreams and drop out of college or law school for a boy. It would kill her. She would regret it later and Mike would regret it too.

Next, he wrote the most absurd insinuation that Zola was so wrapped up in Mike that she wasn't concentrating on her studies and her grades were already suffering. Her father made his case so well, even Zola felt bad for the imaginary girl in question. In the end, he begged Mike to take the money, make something of himself, and not let Zola destroy her life with futile dreams.

Her fingers shook as she threw the letter to the floor. "Oh my God." She jerked her gaze to Mike's. "Those were all lies."

He frowned. "What do you mean?"

"I mean I never said or felt those things. He made it all up. And even if I had thought of leaving school to be with you, I never would've told my dad." Her voice hitched. "He lied. He made up the entire thing to get you to break up with me. And he won." She grabbed Mike's biceps with both hands, rising onto her knees to crawl closer and shake him.

He still frowned.

"He won. He ruined us. He lied to you and convinced you to stop talking to me while at the same time he convinced me you weren't worth it if you couldn't even be bothered to write back to me.

"I was so extremely distraught over your lack of communication that I told him about us one night. Why did I do that?" She wanted to scream. She *was* screaming. "And then…" She sobbed, fighting to continue to speak. "And then while he had you convinced to leave me alone, he conned me into thinking you weren't worth it if you didn't even care I was dating someone else. He told me I'd feel better if I had closure. If I let you go. He made me believe it was the best choice for *me*. But he set us both up, knowing you wouldn't respond to that final email either." Another sob. Another drag of oxygen. She'd never get a full breath again.

Mike grabbed her waist and held her firmly.

"He won. He got exactly what he wanted." Her voice fell as she lowered her butt to her heels. She released his biceps with one hand to slap a palm over her forehead. "I'm so stupid. I let him win."

"Zola, he didn't win, baby. He didn't."

She lifted her gaze to his again, her eyes widening. "How do you figure? I haven't seen you for twelve years. I've never had a healthy normal relationship. I've never even been with another man. I'd say he fucking won."

Mike shook his head. "I'm here now. I don't deserve you, but if you'll have me, I'm here now. I'm a jerk for ever letting this happen between us. I take full responsibility for my actions. I was eighteen, hardly more than a kid, but I knew one thing—I didn't want to jeopardize your relationship with your father. He's all you had. You loved him."

She couldn't speak.

He lowered his voice. "I know you still do. I knew everything he asked of me was fucked up, but I also knew I would forever destroy your bond with him if I showed you that letter. You might have resented me in the long run for ruining your relationship with your dad.

"I was afraid he would disown you if you stayed with me, leave you with nothing. And I had nothing to give you. I had no way to support you. I was broke and uneducated and eighteen. You had everything going for you—a father who loved you, money, great educational opportunities. I couldn't take the risk that you would throw that all away for me."

Her chest tightened.

"Zola, I loved you so much that I let you go. It was the wrong choice. I know that now, but I had only the best intentions when I let you go. It hurt like hell. I never got over it. But I knew after I read that letter from your father I had no other choice. My hands were tied."

More tears slid down her face. She opened her mouth, but no words came out. *He loved me.*

"I can never express how sorry I am."

"Why didn't you tell me all this yesterday or the day before?"

"Because I was a coward. I wanted you to be safe more than anything, and I was afraid you would request someone else be put in charge of your protection if I rocked that boat. I don't trust anyone else with your safety."

His shoulders fell. He lowered his voice. "I thought you would hate me for what I did. I wanted to tell you. I started to a dozen times, but then I stopped myself. Every hour with you has been a blessing. I couldn't bring myself to ruin it with this pile of shitty truths." He motioned toward the mess of papers.

That was when he also spotted the gun on the bed. He lifted it, tucked it back into the bag, and lowered the bag to the floor.

His attention came back to her, his hands grasping her arms. "I know I don't deserve your forgiveness, and I will fully understand if you can never get past this, but I'm gonna beg you to stay with me until this threat to your life is over. It would kill me to turn your life over to someone else to protect you."

She frowned. "Why would someone else protect me?"

He scrunched his forehead up to match hers. "I figure you'd rather be anywhere else in the world than with me right now. And I get that, but I'm pleading with you to put your anger aside and let me do my job to keep you safe."

She shook her head, reaching for his chest and flattening her palms on his warm skin. "You better not pass me off to someone else."

Half his mouth curved up in a small smile and he blew out a breath. "Thank you."

She eased her hands up to his shoulders, enjoying the feel of his skin beneath her palms. "Don't leave me," she told his chest. She didn't know for sure how rocky the next few days might be. As she came to grips with everything that had transpired, there would be moments of angst. But she knew one thing for sure, she didn't want another moment of her life wasted fighting with Mike.

Mike pulled her onto his lap, settling her sideways and

cupping the sides of her face to hold her head just right. His gaze never left hers. "I'm not going anywhere. For as long as you'll have me."

She swallowed past the lump in her throat and licked her lips. "Why aren't you pissed? I want to drag my father out of his home and let the bad guys have their way with him. How can you sit there smiling as if you won the lottery?"

"I did. You're the lottery. Maybe I didn't get to claim my prize for a bit longer than planned, but I'm here now. You're mine. You're on my lap, in my head, under my skin. If you'll have me, you're mine, Zola. I win."

She wiggled her hands out from between them and set her palms on his cheeks, lowering her lips to his. She kissed him as if her life depended on it. That wasn't far from the truth. If she released him, she might actually die.

Mike grabbed her waist again, lowering her back to the bed as he continued kissing her, propping himself over her. His palm spread to encompass her entire waist, his fingers brushing against her breast.

She sucked his tongue into her mouth, unable to get enough. A frantic desperation told her to make up for lost time.

She stuffed thoughts of her father and how angry she was out of her mind to concentrate on the man above her that she had loved more than life itself so very long ago. Could she love him like that again now? "Please," she pleaded against his lips. "I need you."

He lifted his face a few inches, searching her eyes.

"I was always yours. He can never take that away. I

don't know how or when I'll be able to forgive him, but I know one thing for sure, I need to forgive *you* and move on. We've been together for two days, and already I know we have to figure this thing out between us. Walking away isn't an option." She gripped his forearms, her nails digging into his skin.

Mike smiled, his face warming. "I don't deserve you," he stated.

"You have me anyway," she whispered.

He straddled her body and dragged her farther across the bed. When he hesitated, she reached around to his tight ass and plucked the towel from his hips. "I need you," she repeated.

She shuddered when his hands reached under her T-shirt and smoothed up her hips and waist, dragging the cotton material with them. And then he whipped the shirt over her head. Still straddling her on his knees, he lowered his lips to hers, nibbling the corners until he broke the connection once again and leaned back.

His gaze was clouded with lust as he cupped her breasts and began to toy with her nipples.

She arched into his hands as the tiny buds stiffened.

"You're so damn sexy, even more than you were when you were eighteen. I wouldn't have thought it was possible."

The same was true of him, but she couldn't form words at the moment. Instead, she squeezed her legs together to fight the growing need between them. It didn't help.

Mike inched his knees down her body until her pussy was exposed, and then he lifted first one knee and then the other to nudge her thighs open and let him nestle between them.

The exposure made her gasp. All the lights were on. His gaze honed in on her center as he reverently stroked her skin so lightly she could hardly feel it. When he spread her lower lips apart, she groaned. "Mike…"

"You're so wet. I haven't touched you, and already you're so wet."

She squirmed.

He set a finger on her clit and flicked it.

She reached for his thighs and grasped them, her fingernails digging into his skin. Suddenly the idea of wasting even one more moment of time being angry with him in this lifetime overwhelmed her. They'd lost so much time. She wouldn't lose another second.

She reached for his arms and tugged at him. "Now, Mike. Please."

He frowned. "In a rush?"

"Yeah. Please, don't make me wait."

Letting her pull him forward, he set his hands on both sides of her head and eased his lean body between her thighs.

She still gripped his wrists as he lodged himself at her entrance. "Now, Mike," she repeated. It seemed urgent that he be inside her.

And then he was. He thrust in all the way to the hilt so fast it took her breath away.

So full. So tight. So good.

He groaned, his head tipping back as he held himself still. Seconds ticked by.

She needed him to move. Every nerve ending in her body needed the friction only he could give. "Mike," she pleaded.

Slowly he pulled out, making her burn. In an instant she was right at the edge of an orgasm.

Her mouth fell open. She couldn't draw in the next breath.

When he slammed back inside for a second time, she screamed as her pussy gripped him so tightly her vision swam. The orgasm was powerful. It consumed her. Pulse after pulse around his cock and through her clit at the same time.

"Baby…" He was looking down at her, but she couldn't see him clearly. His hands were in her hair, his chest pressed against hers. Then his lips were on her cheek, making their way to her ear. His breath made her shudder just like old times. "So. Fucking. Hot."

He moved then, dragging himself out and thrusting back in. But his mouth remained next to her ear where he continued to nibble and murmur. Some of the words she understood. Others were garbled.

She grabbed his waist and held on as if her life depended on it. She hated the moments when he pulled out, separating them from each other.

His words changed to a low moan as he came deep inside her, holding himself lodged tight until he lowered more of his welcome weight over her. His breath was heaving in her ear until he whispered through the inhalations. "I'm crushing you."

"Do not move an inch." She needed the pressure. She

couldn't explain it, but she needed him blanketing her like this. It didn't matter that she was panting in short breaths, he had to stay right where he was.

He lifted his head first, a smile curling his lips. "I don't really want to have to explain to a paramedic why my woman got asphyxiated in my bed."

She giggled. "That's a bit dramatic."

He lifted a brow. "You can hardly speak because you don't have oxygen."

"Fine."

Mike eased out of her and rolled to the side. She scrambled to stay with him, tucking her body against his, her leg between his, her breasts pressed to his side, her arm across his chest. Her head nestled against his shoulder.

He wrapped his giant hand around her and held her close. "I'm right here, baby."

"For how long?" she asked his chest.

"For as long as you'll have me."

A tear slid from her eye. "We lost so much time."

"Hey, focus on the future." He lifted her chin with his free hand until she met his gaze. "It was a blip on the radar. We have seventy more years together."

She forced a smile. "That's optimistic."

He smiled back. "I won't accept less. But first, I need to clean you up, and then we need to sleep. Before we can start that seventy-year path, we have a terrorist group to shut down. So we need to be fresh and alert tomorrow to make that happen sooner rather than later."

She nodded against him but hated when he eased away from her side, leaving her alone on the bed, on her belly.

Her eyes were closed and she held a pillow under her face when a warm cloth touched her skin. "Spread your legs for me, baby." He'd done the same for her yesterday. It had unnerved her then. She refused to let it bother her now.

His caring touch made her fall even harder for him. She'd harbored feelings for him all these years so that it now came naturally, emotions flowing out of her once again like no time had passed.

After he flipped off the lights, he slid into the bed beside her, drew the covers over them, and snuggled against her side, seemingly needing contact as much as she did.

In moments she fell into a deep sleep.

Chapter Twelve

MIKE LEANED ON his elbow and stared down at the woman next to him. She hadn't moved an inch in eight hours. If he was honest, neither had he until he'd woken up several minutes ago.

He didn't want to disturb her yet. He wanted to enjoy looking at her smooth, pale skin. He had always loved her skin, and he let his gaze roam over her backside.

The covers had shifted down in the night, and he took the chance of easing them farther until her ass was revealed. She didn't stir. Her face was away from him, her hair a tangled mess of strawberry-blond curls. He inhaled the scent of her shampoo and fought the moan that lodged in his throat.

Unable to stop himself, he gently set his fingers on her lower back and stroked her skin. Up and down her spine and then over the soft globe of her butt. He knew the moment she came awake by her soft sigh of contentment.

He smiled as he eased a knee between her legs and let his hand roam lower to tease her inner thighs.

She spread wider for him, squirming against the bed.

He dipped one finger between her folds, finding her already soaking wet.

His cock stiffened against her leg as he reached slowly into her pussy and then dragged his finger over her G-spot.

She moaned into the pillow and turned her face toward him. "That's one way to wake me up."

He grinned. "I considered a glass of cold water, but this seemed more humane." He slid his finger out and circled her clit. When she started to roll to her side, he stopped her with the pressure of his arm against her ass. "Don't. Stay where you are."

She stopped wiggling, but her breathing came heavier as she moaned against the pillow.

He stroked a finger over her clit, loving the way it swelled at his touch. When he pressed against it, she flinched. Her body stiffened, her arms tightening around the pillow.

He was so humbled by the fact that she was his. That she'd always been his. This gorgeous creature coming undone at his touch. As he slowly circled her clit, he couldn't help speaking. "I still can't believe you were never with another man. You were always so sure of yourself in high school, particularly when it came to sex and what you wanted from me."

She turned her head slightly to see him better. "No one was you."

He lowered his face, setting his forehead against hers and kissing her nose. For a moment, he pressed his finger against her clit and stilled.

Her eyes rolled back, and she licked her lips. "No one made me ache for their touch like you do. No one looked into my eyes like you do. No one's warm breath in my ear made me so wet I could come from that alone. No one was you..."

He couldn't breathe. Her words meant more to him than she could imagine. And he needed her even more than he had two minutes ago.

He thrust two fingers into her next, making her gasp. And then he set up a pattern of thrusting into her and then sliding those fingers lower to stroke them in a V around her clit. Again and again he did this until she arched her back and called out his name.

Her head lifted off the bed. She drew her knees up under her, pulling her thighs wider to give him better access.

So fucking gorgeous.

He continued to fuck her with his fingers. Faster. Harder. Her words rang out in his head over and over. *No one was you. No one was you.*

She was panting as she set her forehead on the pillow, leaving her butt raised and her back dipped. When she started rocking back into his thrusts, he nearly came against the mattress.

Keeping his hand in place to continue what he'd started, he managed to rise off the bed and climb between her legs. He set his free hand on her lower back to steady her movements and watched as she came undone under him.

Her pussy tightened around his fingers until she finally shattered. A rush of her arousal coated his hand as a low unidentifiable noise came from her throat.

Before the pulsing slowed to a stop, he jerked his fingers out, grasped her hips, and thrust his cock into her warmth.

"Yes," she shouted.

He held on tight and fucked her harder while she somehow managed to use her elbows to keep from rocking away from him.

He slid his hands up to cup her breasts where they swayed against the sheet. As he pinched her nipples, she moaned again.

Damn, she was responsive. He'd never seen a woman this quick to reach the peak of arousal. But then again, he'd never been with the perfect woman before. One whom he was so in sync with that they didn't know where one ended and the other began.

No. That wasn't true. He'd been with her one time. And he had never forgotten the feeling.

His thoughts scattered as his cock grew stiffer. He gritted his teeth to keep from coming too fast. He wanted her to come again with him, and he smoothed one hand down from her tit to her clit to tease the little nub into coming again.

She was right with him, her body tightening with every thrust. The soft noises coming from deep in her throat grew closer together. He held back. Waiting for her. Fucking in and out of her while hanging on by a thread.

Finally, she stopped moving, her entire body rigid with her release, and he let himself go at the same time, spending himself deep inside her until there was nothing left.

He wrapped an arm around her, causing them to both fall to one side when he could no longer hold himself up.

Gasping for air, he brushed her hair from her face and kissed the sweet spot behind her ear. "There are no words," he whispered.

Except there were words. He just wasn't sure she was ready to hear them.

AN HOUR LATER they were showered and dressed and back in the car. As soon as they were on the highway, Mike called Lambert.

He picked up on the first ring. "You safe?"

"Yes. Back on the road. Heading north."

"Good. I don't like what I'm hearing. Intelligence suggests the terrorists are restless. Pissed. Regrouping. Planning."

"Well, they won't be able to find us." Mike stiffened, gripping the steering wheel. He shot Zola a glance, finding her tight-lipped, her eyes wide.

"Let's hope, but keep your phone handy. I'll update you when I hear more."

"'Kay."

"Why?" Zola mumbled beside him.

He grabbed her hand. "Why what?"

"Why is someone after me? This is insane."

"I don't know, babe, but we're going to find out and stop them."

She twisted her body to face him more fully. "Someone wants me dead, Mike. Someone might kill *you* while trying to get to me." She ran a hand through her hair.

How did she suddenly get so frantic? "Zola, babe, you're not going to die." He squeezed her hand and dragged it closer. "I'm not going to let anything happen to you."

Her voice rose. "You can't know that."

"It's what I was hired to do. I'm pretty good at my job." He chuckled, trying to lighten the mood. "I was trained by the best." He attempted to wink at her.

She groaned. "Don't give me some SEAL crap. Everyone can be killed."

"Not me. I've defied death several times in fact." He pumped out his chest in an exaggerated effort to soothe her. When that didn't work, he sobered. "Listen, we're going to figure this out. Let's go through those three cases again."

He didn't honestly believe rehashing the files of the three men she'd helped put in jail would bring them any closer to the answers, but it would give her something to put her mind on instead of the danger she was in.

She tugged her hand free of his, crossed her arms, and slouched in the seat. "Fine. Let's talk. Case number one is Saabiq Aziz. Infiltrated the States on a student visa in 2010 and never left. He's got ties to ISIS."

Mike nodded. "Right. I don't think it's him. Who was the second guy again?"

"Mohammad Johansson. American born. Caucasian. Changed his first name and converted to Islam in his early twenties when his sister was killed in the bombing at the Boston marathon. And then there was—"

"Wait," he interrupted her, "go back. Something's odd

about that one. More so than the other two I mean. His sister was killed by Islamic militants, so he decided to become one? Isn't that a little off?"

She blew out a long breath. "Yeah. You gotta understand, Johansson was a little off. I mean, you do realize every person who plans and executes a mass murder is a little off. Who could possibly begin to understand what goes on in their minds?"

"What was his reasoning? Do you know?"

"Apparently, he was so furious when his sister died that he began to research Islamic beliefs and somehow got so roped in that he eventually joined their cause and was convinced the reason his sister died was because she wasn't a believer."

"What the actual fuck?"

"Yeah. Since she didn't follow the teachings of Islam and pray to Allah, she deserved to die that day. I told you this man wasn't right in the head."

Mike tapped the steering wheel, feeling like this guy was the key. What was his goal? "And he was convicted, right?"

"Yes. He was a copycat, using the same online magazine to build a bomb and then detonating it in the mall two years ago. Twelve people died. He's in for life without parole."

"And his family? Where are they?"

"In hiding. They lost both their children. They don't even speak to reporters."

Hmm. His mind raced. "If you lost both kids, one to one side of Islamic extremists and the other to the enemy, what would you do?"

"Commit suicide?" she suggested.

"Or seek revenge on anyone you could."

She sighed. "You think it could be his parents?"

"I think we don't rule anyone out." He glanced at her to find her chewing her bottom lip. "And your father? He has worked hard to ensure people like Mohammad and Saabiq are prosecuted to the fullest extent of the law in civil courts."

"So my dad voted in favor of stiffer punishment, and I'm a prosecutor…"

"Exactly." Mike reached for his phone and dialed Lambert.

"Dorsen."

"Got an idea. Look into the parents of Mohammad Johansson. He was one of the cases Zola tried and convicted. The mall bombing two years ago."

"On it. What makes you think they're involved?"

"Smells fishy."

"You got it. Later." Lambert hung up.

Mike dialed Tex.

"'Bout time you called. I've been worried."

"Yeah, sorry. We've been on the move."

"Guess the guys you're working for found nothing at my house. I've been watching the surveillance. It's still secure. Your belongings are safe inside. I'd send a cleaning service over, but I wouldn't want to risk anyone's life unnecessarily."

"Don't. Leave it. I'll go back when this is over." He glanced at Zola. "Maybe I can finish my vacation in peace."

Tex chuckled. "Let's hope so. How's Zola holding up?"

"She's right here. You're on speaker."

"I'm hanging in there," Zola told Tex.

"Good. You're in good hands. Stick with Dorsen."

"Plan to." She smiled at Mike, her face warming him from the inside out.

"Listen, Tex. Hate to ask, but can you do some digging for me?"

"Of course. You don't even have to ask. Give it to me."

"My contact is on it too, but I know you're the better hacker. And he works slightly more above the law than you." Mike chuckled, knowing Tex would get more information and faster than anyone working even in a clandestine capacity for the CIA.

Tex laughed again. "Nothing is too hidden for me to get to it. What do you need?"

"Kid named Mohammad Johansson. Zola was on the team with the DA that prosecuted him for the mall shooting two years ago."

"Yep. I remember him. He's in for life, isn't he?"

"Yes. But I have suspicions about his parents."

"Think they might want revenge?"

"That's where my mind is, yes."

"On it. I'll call you when I have something." Tex hung up.

Mike took the next exit and pulled into the parking lot of a fast food chain. "This okay? I'm starving, and I don't want to take too long."

"Of course." She unbuckled her seat belt, but her hands were shaking, and before he opened his car door, he reached for her. Wrapping a hand around the back of her neck, he drew her face closer to his. "You okay?"

"Sure." She nodded with too much force.

"I know it's overwhelming, but we'll get to the bottom of this and catch whoever is after you. Trust me?"

"Seems like I don't have to." She gave him a half smile. "Looks like you have friends in all the right places who have you covered."

"True. But I'm the one next to you with the gun."

"And I haven't forgotten that for a moment."

"Okay. Let's go eat." He pulled her head closer and kissed her lips briefly before releasing her.

Damn, she was fantastic.

ZOLA COULDN'T STOP fidgeting. She'd managed to eat a chicken sandwich and drink a soda, but the fries made her stomach roil. The sandwich was like cardboard in her mouth, but she forced it down.

Now they were back in the car and moving west again. "What difference does it make where we stop? I mean, do we really need to keep running? No one knows where we are, so why does it matter if it's here or Chicago?"

He shot her a glance. "I never intended to go to Chicago."

She rolled her eyes. "I was just tossing out any city west of here."

"Ah. Well, technically it doesn't matter. But I feel more protected when we're on the move. When we stop, we're a bit more exposed."

She took several deep breaths, trying to put her thoughts into words. "I don't know why, but I feel nervous. I'm worried about my dad. I'm afraid this has more to do with him than with me."

"I can understand that."

She was pissed at her father, but that didn't mean she wasn't concerned about him at the same time. "What's wrong with me? The man paid my boyfriend to break up with me. I should shoot him myself."

Mike didn't say a single word. Minutes went by.

Zola freaked out a bit at his silence.

Finally, he took the next exit and pulled into a gas station. He jumped from the car and set the pump up, and then he was back. He turned his body her direction and took both her hands. "Babe, your dad will always be your dad. I would never in this lifetime suggest that you harbor anger toward him. I'd be the last man to suggest that."

She winced. "Because you don't know your parents?"

"Exactly. I'd give anything to have a terrible relationship with my father. At least I would know who he was. I don't remember my dad. He died when I was too young. Maybe he was a jackass." He shrugged. "Maybe he was a good guy. I'll never know. But he was killed, and I'd love to have an hour to argue with him if it meant I got to see him."

"That makes sense." It broke her heart that Mike didn't have either parent.

"So, no matter what happens, I will always encourage you to keep an open mind and maintain contact with your dad. He made choices I don't agree with. So did I. So did you. We all have to get past this. Maybe he'll be more accepting of me after all these years. In either case, I would hope you would stay with me this time and not let him tear us apart, but that doesn't mean I want you to stop speaking to him or seeing him.

"I will always encourage you to make every attempt to fix things. Maybe he's genuinely sorry for his efforts when we were teenagers. Maybe he's a new man. If so, great. If not, we'll find a way to deal.

"I feel confident he'll eventually come around. You're his daughter. His only child. He won't let you slip away over something as petty as being in a relationship with a foster kid with a master's degree in biology who's served two tours with the SEALs." He winked.

She smiled and inhaled slowly. "Thank you."

"For what?"

"For being so damn supportive."

He shrugged as if it were no big deal when he knew damn good and well it meant everything to her.

After a quick peck on the lips, he exited the car to remove the pump, and then they were on the road again.

She stared out the windshield for a long time before speaking again. "Do you really think we can make things work between us?"

He flinched, glancing her direction. "Of course. Why the hell not?"

She shrugged. "We've been together like three days. Under intense circumstances."

He chuckled, startling her. "You gonna start quoting Sandra Bullock now?"

She giggled for the first time in hours. Or had it been longer?

He set a hand on her thigh. "If so, and you're worried about a relationship based on an intense experience, we could base it on sex instead."

She laughed again, harder. "Be serious, will you? I'm legitimately concerned. I mean, we haven't seen each other for twelve years and then boom. You're back. We pick up like we never separated, and then we live in crisis mode, having sex occasionally on the side. How is this a good way to start out?"

"First of all, you make it sound like we had nothing to begin with. I was in love with you when I last saw you. So, it's more like the relationship has been on hold all these years. I never stopped loving you."

She stopped breathing because she agreed with his assessment.

He continued, "And second of all, the sex is amazing, so you can't possibly be flippant about that aspect. Unless all those orgasms you've screamed out under my control were faked." He sent her a wide grin, his eyebrows lifted.

"So now we're switching from Sandra Bullock to Meg Ryan?" She fought the urge to laugh. "I don't fake orgasms."

"Babe, apparently you haven't even *had* any orgasms."

"I never said that," she teased. "I simply haven't had any with a man."

"Semantics. And I'm still trying to keep from pumping my chest out at that revelation."

"How cocky."

"What would you expect?"

She rolled her eyes. "Okay. You're right. I pined after you and couldn't bring myself to sleep with another man. Could we not dwell on that?"

"Sure. I mean I'll try not to bring it up more than once or twice a day for the next seventy years."

Several seconds of silence sobered her.

"What are you thinking?" he asked.

"That I live in Connecticut, and I don't even know where you live."

He sighed. "I don't know either. Until I take my next assignment. I go where the FBI tells me."

"For how long?"

"For as long as it takes to solve the case. I was in Chicago for over a year. Longest case I've been on. Some are short. Others seem to take forever."

"And when you're assigned to a city like that, can you travel back and forth to wherever home is?"

He winced as she stared at him. "No. Not usually."

She continued to look at him. How the hell would that work between them?

"Babe, we don't have to figure everything in the world out today."

"Yeah, but this is a big one. You work for the FBI. I work for the district attorney. I love my job. It's fulfilling. It changes lives."

"I'd like to think mine changes lives too. Saves them," he countered.

She nodded slowly. This could put them at an impasse. Under no circumstances could she visualize quitting her job, especially to become an unemployed wife always on the fringe, unable to work because her husband worked for the FBI and she needed to stay low.

Was it possible her dad had a point all along? Maybe he didn't want her to fall into a situation where she gave up everything for a man. The problem was that she was smart enough to know that herself. She didn't need him to tell her. Not a chance in hell would she give up her dreams for someone else.

Would she have felt the same way a decade ago? If she had maintained a relationship with Mike, would he have eventually worn her down until she left law school or even the state to follow him where his dreams led?

She shuddered.

"Zola, you're worrying too hard. Don't get so far ahead of things. We just got back together. Don't dwell on the future yet."

"So, you're suggesting we ignore our differences and concentrate on the good sex for a while until it gets harder and harder to face reality?"

His face drew up in a frown. He pursed his lips, saying nothing else for a long time.

She leaned back in the seat, tipping her head toward the headrest and closing her eyes. Why did she pick a fight with him? It wasn't necessary. They both had their jobs, their convictions. They weren't so different from each other.

But she couldn't shake the feeling that if she'd stayed with him all those years ago, she would have given up her dreams for him, and they would have ended up torn apart.

Nothing had really changed since then.

When they were sixteen and they first started talking, they'd been drawn together for the simple reason that they were both driven and hardworking. Those same aspects also made them incompatible.

After a few more miles, Mike pulled off the highway in a small town.

"Why are we stopping?"

It was early. Not even dinner time. His voice was softer than usual. "Like you said, no reason to keep moving. We can stop for the night and relax for a while. Watch some TV. Get a nice dinner."

She knew it was more than that, but she didn't say anything.

Fifteen minutes later, they opened the door of their room on the third floor and locked themselves inside.

Zola dropped their bags on the floor next to the ones Mike dropped. "We're going to need to do laundry soon or buy more clothes."

"Yeah." He didn't meet her gaze. In fact, he hadn't since things got tense between them. He headed for the bathroom. "Mind if I shower first? I feel like I walked here."

"Of course. Go ahead." Her heart fell a bit at the awkwardness between them, but she didn't want to show it.

He stepped into the bathroom with the bag of toiletries and closed the door with a snick that made her jump where she still stood next to the entrance.

Damn. Why did she have to push things? They'd been getting along so well. Now she'd put a strain on their relationship. On the other hand, she hadn't pointed out anything that wasn't true. It might be hard to face, but sooner or later, they were going to have to admit they had serious life commitments that didn't mesh.

The water came on, and she shuffled across the room to turn on the television. She paid no attention as she flipped from one channel to the next.

By the time Mike stepped out of the bathroom, she had the TV running on mute on a random channel, and she lay propped up against the headboard of the king-size bed.

"Nothing interesting on?" he asked.

"No. How was the shower?"

"Good pressure. The showerhead isn't high enough, but I'm used to that."

She watched as he rummaged through their bags, grabbing a pair of boxers and then dropped his towel to shrug into them. His firm ass was in her line of vision.

Damn, he was nice to look at. She admired every single ripple of muscle up his back and down his legs. From behind she couldn't see the scars on his knee that told the tale of his injuries.

When he turned around, he stalked directly toward her.

She wasn't sure of his intentions, but he didn't take his gaze off her as he climbed onto the bed, kneeled in front of her crossed legs, and set his hands on the headboard at her sides. "We need to talk."

"Yeah." Should she put it off for a while longer? Go take a shower? She lowered her gaze to his chest, which was a mistake. It made her lick her lips, wetness pooling in her panties.

"Zola, look at me."

She lifted her face, feeling the flush that raced up her cheeks.

"Not gonna give you up without a fight."

She didn't know how to process that. What did he mean?

"We're meant to be together. I know it in my soul. I won't let you go over something as petty as location. We will figure this out."

She nodded, not believing it with as much certainty as him. She couldn't imagine how they were going to work out their geographical differences. "I should shower."

"You should talk to me."

"I don't know what else there is to say. I live in Connecticut, and you don't even know where you live. But it's not Connecticut."

He frowned.

"The reality is that if either of us gave up our jobs for the other, there would be resentment that lasted a lifetime."

"I think you're putting the cart before the horse, babe."

She shook her head. "I think you're delusional if you refuse to face the facts." She slid under his arm and padded toward the bathroom without a backward glance. She needed to be alone for a while anyway and intended to fill the bathtub and soak in it instead of standing in the shower.

The warm water should have been soothing, but arguing with Mike made her uneasy in a way that caused her heart to ache. She started this disagreement. And why? So she could be right about something? Was it necessary for her to be right about this topic? It would suck if her theory proved correct.

On the one hand, she couldn't imagine how they would work out their living arrangements. On the other hand, she also couldn't visualize a life without him now that she had him back.

After twelve years without a word, not knowing where he was or if he was alive or dead, in just days she was attached to him with a stronger bond than they'd had in their teens.

It would take courage and hard work to pull off a relationship with him, but was she willing to throw everything away without trying? Hell no.

She climbed out of the tub, dried off, and wrapped a towel around her body. With a deep breath, intending to apologize for her temporary insanity, she opened the door and stepped into the main room.

Her breath whooshed from her body when she found the curtains pulled to block out most of the late-afternoon rays and Mike on his side in the middle of the bed, completely naked. He leaned his head casually against his palm, his other hand resting gently across his thigh.

But more importantly, it was difficult to take her gaze off his thick length.

She swallowed. "I was going to say I was sorry."

"Me too." His voice was low. Sexy.

"My fault. I brought it up. You're right. I'm getting ahead of myself."

He shook his head. "No. You have a good point. We need to be open with each other and discuss our options. I know it's only been a few days, but I know in my heart I want to make things work between us." He lifted his hand off his thigh and reached out. "Come here."

She eased across the floor toward him and dropped the towel when she reached the bed.

His smile grew.

"We haven't even had dinner yet," she whispered as she crawled onto the bed.

He lifted a brow. "Is there a rule that says people must eat dinner before having sex?"

She giggled. "No. I'm just thinking about how absorbed we get and what the chances are we would ever come up for air and eat later."

He shrugged. "If I miss a meal, it will be worth it."

She smiled broader. "True."

"Besides, I'm more interested in eating *you* than anything else."

A flush covered her face and rushed down her chest.

Mike's hand snaked out, grabbed her around the waist, and lowered her onto her back next to him. He looked down at her face as he leaned over her. "So sexy. You take my breath away." And those were the last few words uttered between them for several hours.

She was right. They ended up calling for Chinese takeout after the sun went down.

And she was not sorry.

Chapter Thirteen

"WHAT TIME IS it?" Zola muttered groggily as she lifted her head from the car door, wincing at the crick in her neck. "How long was I asleep?"

"About an hour. You must have been exhausted. It's two o'clock."

She rubbed her neck, feeling the twinge of pain as it raced down her back. How had she slept so hard in such an uncomfortable position?

She glanced out the window, trying to figure out where they were. They hadn't spoken about it, but she noticed they were heading slowly toward Connecticut. They took backroads and moved in no rush.

Mike's phone rang, startling her.

He connected through the Bluetooth. "Tex. Whatcha got for me?"

"You were right."

Zola sat up straighter, her spine going rigid.

Tex continued, "The Johanssons aren't quite right. They're living under the radar, but they aren't simply hiding from the press because they are regular grieving parents. They've have contacts with the extremists."

"You're sure?" Mike asked.

"Oh yeah. Most of their email correspondence is with a well-known terrorist organization operating in the Northeast. They want revenge for the death of their daughter and the incarceration of their son."

"And they think they will get that if they take more lives?" Mike's frustration was evident in his tone.

"Would seem that way. They have been following the senator's movements for months. And recently added Zola when they realized she was on the prosecuting team and hurting her could get to her father. Chances are they decided she was an easier target than the senator. Richard Carver isn't as easy to attack."

"Shit." Mike slammed his palm on the steering wheel, making Zola flinch.

She reached across the center of the car and set her hand on his thigh. "This is good news," she told him. "At least we know who we're looking for and what we're dealing with."

Tex barked out sharp laughter. "Your woman has a point there."

Zola smiled. Even though she hadn't met Tex and possibly never would, she knew she liked him.

Mike groaned. "Thanks, man. I owe you one. I owe you several. Go back to your wife. I'll turn this info over to my contact."

"Wish I knew who that was. My curiosity is forever piqued."

"Your safety is my primary concern," Mike told Tex.

"Bah. I've been in tighter situations than you'll ever see," he joked. "And I only have one leg."

Mike grinned. "Okay, let's not get into which one of us is gimpier. You'll always win. My bum knee doesn't compare."

Zola couldn't help but smile. Yeah, she liked Tex a lot. The more she learned about him, the more she knew she would love him. Whoever he was married to hit the jackpot.

She glanced at Mike, knowing she too had hit the jackpot.

Mike ended the call and placed another call.

"Dorsen. I don't have much to tell you yet." This came from the voice of Mike's contact.

"That's okay. I pulled some strings, called in a favor. It's the parents. They're involved."

"Shit."

Zola personally didn't believe any favor had been called with Tex. Instead, she could tell the two of them would do anything for the other and probably dozens of others simply because they had been active SEALs at one point. SEALs tended to stick together for life, even when they weren't on the same team and had never met. Didn't matter. If one of them needed help, they would all jump to the aid of their brethren.

Mike relayed the information to his contact, who promised to get some people on the Johanssons immediately.

"Don't let them know you're watching them, and don't

approach them. I don't want to give away our knowledge of their involvement and risk them going dark. I'm not convinced they're the ones following Zola or perhaps her father. I'm going to bet they're part of a larger organization that has the manpower to take down even a senator. We need to tread carefully."

"Of course. I'll keep things low. Watch the Johanssons and see if they make any more moves. If I find out anything, I'll let you know."

"Thanks." Mike ended the call, and she watched him lift and lower his shoulders several times, his hands at ten and two on the steering wheel.

"You're going after them, aren't you?"

He shot her glance. "What are you, psychic?"

She smiled. "I know you, Mike. You aren't the sort of man to sit back and wait to see what happens. You're a man of action. You've had us aimed for New Haven this entire time."

"Yeah, well, I have another person to consider now. It would be stupid of me to put your life in danger while I pursue the enemy at close range."

"Who are you trying to convince?" She tried not to laugh.

He ignored her question and glanced out the rearview mirror instead.

Surely they weren't being followed. "What's the matter, Mike? Talk to me."

"Nothing. Just thinking. Staying diligent."

Uh-huh. That was so like him. *Not.*

The next time they stopped for gas Zola asked Mike if

he wanted her to drive awhile. Every time she offered he turned her down.

"I got it. Your job is to keep me entertained." He led her back to the car with a hand on the small of her back, as usual. Before he unlocked the car, he also leaned down, brushed her hair away, and kissed the sensitive spot behind her ear.

She set her forehead against his chest and fisted his T-shirt at the sides. "Shouldn't you let your boss handle this?"

"Yep."

"Then what are we doing?" She lifted her face. "What's your plan?"

"I don't know, babe. I just know I need to be closer. If those idiots plan to do something, I don't want to be halfway across the country when they act."

"Do what? I mean, if it's me they're targeting, how can they possibly act if they don't know where I am?" The moment the words left her mouth she knew. "Oh. Right. My dad. You think they will go after him."

He nodded. "I'm sure of it. We still don't know if they're targeting you to get to him, targeting him to get to you, or if they simply don't give a fuck who they target as long as they get revenge."

She shuddered, pressing her body against his. "What's wrong with people?"

"I don't know, Zola. It's a mystery."

When they were back in the car, Mike adjusted the rearview mirror for the millionth time and then took off.

Moments later, she saw him tense and glanced out the back window.

Surely he was being paranoid. No way in hell would the enemy be that obvious. But as he turned first one corner then another, she had her doubts. The black, nondescript four-door behind them followed. Not close. Not far.

She said nothing, glancing at Mike every few seconds.

After taking another left turn, he stiffened. "Zola," he began in the calmest voice she'd ever heard. "We're being followed."

"I see that."

"I need you to brace yourself. I'm going to make some sharp turns to shake them."

She turned her head to look out the back again and then righted herself and flattened one hand on the dash.

He hit the gas, speeding down the road until he came to the first corner. As he rounded it, the tires of the car behind them squealed.

Two more turns and she noticed a sign for the highway entrance up ahead.

The car was gaining on them.

Mike lifted his hips, reached to the small of his back, and tugged his gun free of his jeans. He tucked it between his thighs. "Can you shoot, Zola?"

She gasped. "What? No, I can't shoot a gun." She tried to sound calm, but failed.

"It's okay. Don't worry. I'm a good shot." He gave a fake chuckle. "If you want, there's a Ruger in my backpack behind the seat. It's easy to handle."

"Shit. No." She was shaking. "I don't know the first thing about guns, Mike. I can't do it."

"Okay. It's okay." He swerved hard as he entered the

highway. The black car followed.

When he floored the pedal, they were both thrown against the seat. "Hold on." He jerked the steering wheel to the left and moved across the lines of traffic. There wasn't much, thank God. It was the middle of the day. Most people were at work.

Their tail remained but didn't attempt to shoot at them nor try to ram them or drive them off the road. Small blessings.

They were going dangerously fast now. "Come on. Come on," he muttered, scanning the side of the highway. "What we need is a cop," he stated under his breath.

She had no idea how that was going to be helpful, but she continued to grip the dash and the console.

Suddenly, flashing lights filled her vision on the side of the highway.

"Hold on," Mike shouted.

She braced herself for whatever he had in mind a moment before he swerved into the center lane and hit the brakes. The car tailing them kept going right on by.

The police vehicle was far behind them, still picking up momentum. It had been parked on the side of the highway with no chance to get up to the speed needed to catch either vehicle speeding by quick enough.

Mike was now traveling at a regular speed between the fuckers who had been tailing them and the police. He surprised her when he quickly veered into the far right lane, exited the highway, and made a quick left to go under the overpass, stopping at the red light.

Zola was holding her breath.

"We lost them." He reached across the center of the car and set his hand on her thigh. "We're okay." She flinched.

"You didn't stop for the cops." Her voice was high-pitched. She glanced around to look out the back window.

"Yeah, that would've caused a lot of red tape. Don't worry. I'll have someone call it in and let them know what they were pursuing.

She was shaking uncontrollably. "How did they find us?"

"No idea. But I want to keep moving, and I need to call my contact." He hit a few buttons on his phone before pulling back onto the highway going the other direction.

"Dorsen. What's the latest?"

"Someone found us."

"Shit. Where?"

"We were followed after we stopped for gas. How the fuck did anyone know where we were?" He slammed a hand on the steering wheel. "They have to be tracking us somehow."

"Where are you?" Mike's contact sounded concerned even to Zola's ears.

"Heading north on Highway 8 now. Have someone call the locals and let them know what they failed to catch southbound at exit forty-four."

"Did you get plates?"

"Nope. Black Nissan Sentra. No front plates. Lost it when the cops turned their lights on."

"I'm calling now. You need to ditch the car again."

"Obviously, but you need to fucking figure out how we were found. I don't like this."

Zola gripped the console with her fingers, her heart pounding. *If they found us once, they could find us again...*

"I'll call you back in five. Stay diligent."

As Mike picked up speed on the highway again, Zola kept her gaze all around them. She didn't want to distract him, but she had about a million questions.

Ten minutes went by. She had finally begun to relax marginally when Mike sat up straighter. "Shit," he muttered. His gaze was on the rearview mirror again.

Zola twisted around to glance out the rear window. "What now?"

"We have another tail."

"Are you sure?" She could only see two cars behind them, both at a reasonable distance.

"Yes. The silver car on our ass has been there for a while. I wasn't too worried about it by itself. Until I started slowing down and speeding up."

"What do you mean?"

"The driver is pacing me. He slows and speeds to remain behind me."

"You're sure?"

"I am now that his friend has arrived." Mike flexed his fingers on the steering wheel.

Zola glanced out the back again. "His friend? The other car? The blue one?"

"Yeah. It showed up next to the silver one a few minutes ago. They're both pacing me, and they surely know that I'm aware." Mike drove faster.

The two cars kept up.

Zola grabbed the dashboard. "What do we do?"

"Outrun them." He went faster.

"How far to the next exit? Can we get off? Should we call the police?" She started shaking. This wasn't good.

"Call 911, baby."

She grabbed his phone from his lap. Before she had time to hit the buttons, the two cars were right on their tail. The blue sedan suddenly burst forward, aligning itself on Mike's side of the car.

She stared out the window in horror, her fingers shaking, forcing her to glance down and dial.

"Hold on, Zola," Mike shouted as the blue car slammed into his door.

Just as she placed the call, the phone went flying out of her hand to land somewhere in the back seat.

"Fuck." Mike swerved onto the shoulder and then glanced her direction. "You okay?"

"Yes." She wasn't. Not by a long shot. She was scared out of her mind. And she couldn't reach the phone. She hoped to God the operator could track it somehow and find them.

Mike righted them back onto the highway, jerking the steering wheel so hard that he hit the blue sedan near the front passenger tire.

The jolt shoved Zola forward. She hit her head on the dashboard. Not hard enough to give her a concussion, but it smarted, and she grabbed onto the handle above the doorframe with one hand, bracing herself against the dash with her other.

They were going so fast. She twisted around to find the silver car right on their bumper. With the blue car boxing them in at the side, there was nowhere to go. "Mike?"

"Fuck," he screamed again. "Fuck. They're going to shove us off the road."

"Can you outrun them?"

"Not in this car. I'm going as fast as I can." He held the steering wheel so tightly his fingers were white.

The blue car slammed into his side again.

Zola screamed.

Mike lost control, careening off the side of the road.

She looked out the front windshield only to discover they were on a steep embankment. The car leaned hard to her side, tipping on two wheels. She was thrown violently into the door, screaming.

Before she could get her bearings, the car rolled her direction. "*Mike*," she shouted, but she had no idea if he heard her. She felt like a rag doll being tossed every direction, the seat belt locking and keeping her from hitting the roof or slamming into Mike.

As the car once again landed upright, it continued to plow forward. She tried to grab onto anything, but her arms were flailing around. Her screams grew louder as she saw them heading directly toward a tree. "*Mike*."

He still didn't respond, and they were moving so erratically that she couldn't get her head to turn his direction. At the last second before they hit the tree, she threw her arms across her face on instinct.

The crash was loud, the sound of glass shattering and metal buckling deafening. And then it was over. Silence.

She lowered her arms and turned toward Mike. He was slumped her direction, his head leaning too far. Blood ran down his face.

"*Mike!*" She reached for him, unable to do much with her seat belt still choking her. "Dammit, Mike. Talk to me." She tugged on the seat belt, pushing the release button with shaky fingers. Finally, it let her go.

Gasping for oxygen, she tried to right his head. It was too heavy. Dead weight. In a panic, she screamed again. "Oh God. Mike. Wake up." Was he even alive?

Suddenly her car door jerked open.

For a split second she was relieved, thinking someone was there to help, but then an arm reached in and grabbed her by the wrist. "Stop. We need to help him. Call 911." She twisted to look at the person leaning into the car and stopped breathing.

This man wasn't there to help her. He was the man who ran them off the road. Tall. Thick. Dark. Under normal circumstances, he could be considered attractive. She could tell by the scowl on his face that he didn't give a fuck about Mike. And he confirmed that when he yanked her out of the car so hard her arm nearly came out of the socket.

Before she could catch her breath, he wrapped his forearm around her waist and lifted her off the ground. Her back was pressed against his side as he rushed up the embankment.

She flailed her arms and legs, kicking and screaming. Her hair was in total disarray around her face, making it difficult to see.

He seemed undaunted by her attempt to break free. He raced up the hill to the highway, and before she could protest further, she was shoved into the backseat of the silver car. She reached out with both hands and feet to stop the motion, but he easily tucked her into the car.

Someone else was inside. Hands reached out to grab her, dragging her the rest of the way in and shoving her to the floor. The door slammed behind her, sealing her fate. A foot landed on her back, pushing her face toward the floorboard.

She couldn't breathe. She fought with every ounce of energy she had, jerking around to get out from under the pressure on her spine. When she reared back, lifting her face far enough to see over the edge of the window, a fist slammed into her temple.

She felt the impact, knew her head ricocheted off the back of the seat. And then nothing…

SO MUCH PAIN…

Zola cringed when she tried to open her eyes. So dark. Where was she? What happened?

She blinked as she attempted to lift her arms. She tugged on her wrists only to discover they were trapped at the small of her back. Tied together.

Her eyes shot open wide. She tried to scream next, but no sound came out. Her mouth was taped shut. Panic set in. She was jolted back and forth several times before she realized she was in the trunk.

Fuck.

The car was moving and she was in the trunk. She could hear faint voices coming from the front of the car. It sounded like two people were arguing in another language.

Her memory flooded back.

The accident.

No, it wasn't an accident. Someone had intentionally run Mike off the road.

Mike. Oh, God. Was he okay?

She tugged on her arms again, reaching with her fingers to figure out what was trapping her wrists. Duct tape. Probably also covering her mouth.

An attempt to move her legs proved they too were taped together at the ankles and the knees.

She started to hyperventilate, unable to draw enough oxygen into her nose. If she didn't calm down, she would die in the trunk. This was not how she wanted to die. She needed to fight.

For Mike. She had to believe he was okay. These men didn't want him. They wanted her. Hopefully he had simply been knocked out, and they'd left him there. But how long would it take someone to find him? Could anyone even detect the accident from the highway? They'd gone down an embankment and rolled to a stop, hitting a tree. She prayed someone saw the accident. Or maybe the 911 call connected.

She took deep breaths in through her nose, her chest heaving. Closing her eyes, she forced herself to calm. Should she wiggle around and kick out the taillights? She'd seen people do it in movies.

It didn't matter. She didn't have enough space to move and no way to get the right angle to kick anything. She had no leverage, and her arms were screaming with the pain of being wrenched behind her too far. How long had she been knocked out?

Her head pounded. If she didn't have a concussion from the accident, she surely suffered one when the man in the backseat slammed his fist into the side of her head.

Her right eye was swollen and stiff. Dried blood? She had no idea how badly she'd been hurt in the crash with no time to assess her injuries before she was yanked out of the car and forced up the hill.

The vehicle slowed, making her hold her breath. It took a turn and kept going. She realized she would rather they didn't reach their destination. The longer they were in the car, the longer she was alive.

Another turn. And then another. They weren't going as fast anymore. They had to be in a city or suburbs somewhere.

It was difficult to concentrate on anything. She tried to memorize the turns, but what good would it do her with no point of reference?

Suddenly she rocked forward as the car went over a bump of some sort. A curb? And then it angled uphill for a few seconds. Another jolt and then it seemed as though they were no longer on the road. She was tossed around ruthlessly as the car continued to move over an uneven surface. Not gravel. She couldn't hear the crunch. Grass? Dirt?

When it stopped, she felt a new wave of panic. Where were they? Would they kill her here? Maybe they had gone off the road a ways to dump her body.

Shouting came from outside, both sides of the car and

someone else from farther away.

Maybe she should pretend to be passed out.

Before she could make a decision, the trunk flew open and huge hands reached in to grab her by the shoulders.

Her eyes were wide, and she tried to scream, but the tape muffled any sound. This was the same man who had grabbed her from the car earlier. He hefted her up by the waist and tossed her over his shoulder.

With no care for her comfort, he trudged away from the car while speaking in what she assumed was Arabic to someone else.

She had no way to brace herself, so her head slammed into his back repeatedly, her hair hanging in a riot of clumps, blocking her vision.

He climbed a few steps and a door opened. Bright lights assaulted her as he stepped inside. She hit her head on the doorframe. He didn't care or didn't notice, but a new bump swelled instantly next to her swollen eye.

More voices came from someplace else in the house. Shouting. Mostly in Arabic, but someone was speaking English.

She knew that voice…

Noooo!

Her father. She was in her childhood home.

Chapter Fourteen

MIKE GROANED. EVERYTHING hurt. He forced his eyes open to find several people leaning over him. "What happened?" His voice was so weak he wasn't sure anyone heard him.

"You were in an accident, sir. Try to remain still. We're going to get you to a hospital."

Accident…

He shoved the hands in front of him away and bolted upright on the gurney. "Where's Zola?" he shouted, jerking his head around to search for her. "*Zola.*" His voice rose. Where the fuck was she?

"Sir, I need you to calm down." Hands shoved him, trying to get him to lie back.

"Where is she?" He pushed the man away, flung his legs over the side of the gurney, and jumped to the ground. Gasping at the incredible sharp pain at the front of his head, he spun around. They were on the side of the highway. He glanced down the embankment to see his car at the bottom, a twisted heap of metal that had come to rest upright wrapped around a tree.

"Sir. Please sit down. You're injured."

"Where's Zola?" He spun to face the two men who approached him with their palms open and stretched out.

The man on the right furrowed his brow. "Who's Zola?"

"My girlfriend. She was with me? Did she… Is she…?" He panicked. Was she dead? Surely someone would tell him if she hadn't made it. He turned to race back down the hill, but both men lurched forward and grabbed him by the arms.

The man on the right spoke again. "There was no one with you, sir."

He froze. "What?" He whirled around to stare at the paramedics, noticing there were several firemen and a few police officers close by also. He glanced at about eight blank faces, each of them confused.

Finally, an officer came forward. "There was someone with you?"

Mike closed his eyes, pressing his forehead against his fingers. *Fuck.* He jerked his face back up. "Yes. They took her."

"Who?" the officer asked.

"The men who ran us off the road." He spun around again, looking for any evidence of the other cars. The struggle. Anything.

"Someone ran you off the road?" the officer asked.

"Jesus. We have to hurry." Mike rushed forward, pausing for a moment to grab the edge of the gurney and brace himself as he felt faint. He had to pull it together and find her.

"Sir?" the officer asked.

"Which car is yours?" Mike returned. "I need you to get me someplace. And I need a phone."

"Sir, you're injured," one of the paramedics said. "We need to get you to the hospital."

"Not a chance." Mike faced the officer instead. "You drive. I'll talk on the way."

The officer hesitated.

Mike's voice rose. "She's in danger. This is important." He suddenly remembered who he was and reached into his back pocket to pull out his wallet. Flipping it open, he held it out for the officer to see. "I'm with the FBI." He was so totally not working for the FBI today, nor was his current assignment even known to the FBI, but he'd needed to say something to get the officer to move.

"Okay." The guy nodded and turned around. "Let's go."

Voices of shock filled the air behind him. He ignored all of them as he jogged toward the police car. "What time is it?" He needed to establish how long he'd been out.

"Five o'clock."

Awhile then. He tugged the passenger door open and folded himself inside as the cop did the same and then pulled away from the curb. "You going to tell me where I'm going and what this is about?"

"I need your phone," Mike stated. He had no idea where his was. Zola had been using it. It probably got thrown from the car.

The officer handed him a phone.

With shaky fingers, Mike forced himself to calm down enough to remember the number and then dial.

Two rings. Three. Four. Finally an answer. "Hello?"

"Greg."

"Dorsen? Oh my God. Where are you?"

"Police car. They took Zola. They *took* her," he shouted. "Two cars tailed us. How the fuck did they find us? They ran us off the highway, and when I came to, she was gone." He rambled all that so rapidly Lambert didn't have a chance to get a word in.

"Okay. Listen to me. They have her father too."

"*Fuck*," he shouted.

"They're holding him hostage in his home. No idea how long it's been, but he didn't show up for work today, and the FBI discovered he was being held hostage about an hour ago."

"Wasn't anyone guarding him?"

"Yes. Sliced throat. And they found his butler unconscious on the front steps."

"Fuck," Mike muttered again, punching the dashboard as the officer driving the car flinched. Mike turned to face the man, rattling off the address of Zola's father. Then he turned his attention back to Lambert. "Have they made any demands?"

"Not yet. Hold on. If I lose you, I'll call you back."

Seconds ticked by. Mike could do nothing but wait and listen to the silence.

Finally, Greg was back. "The same people have Zola. They must have brought her to her father's home. My men spotted them carrying her into the back of the house two minutes ago."

"*Fuck*." The one word came out as a scream. He didn't care that he was being repetitive. "Can you drive any faster, man?" he asked the officer.

The guy nodded and hit the gas, turning on his lights and siren. Luckily he never balked at the fact that they were nearly an hour from New Haven.

"Tell me what I'm facing," Mike said to Lambert.

"House is surrounded. SWAT. FBI. Police. It's all over the news by now. We're pretty sure there were two men inside holding Senator Carver, and two men showed up with Zola."

"But someone saw her right? She was alive?"

"Appeared that way, yes."

"How did they get past the police to enter the house?"

"The men inside hauled the senator to the door with a gun to his head, threatening to shoot him on the spot if they didn't break lines and let the car through."

"Dammit." Mike squeezed his eyes shut and rubbed his forehead. Flecks of blood fell off like dandruff to land on his lap. He had no idea how injured he was, but he didn't feel anything wet indicating an open wound. "ETA?" he asked the driver.

"Forty-five minutes."

"I can't be seen, Dorsen. And you don't exist."

"Right. Well, I exist as Zola's boyfriend, an FBI agent on vacation, and a former SEAL."

"True. Go get her."

Mike ended the call, dropping the phone in his lap as he took deep breaths and thought of a plan.

"Your girlfriend is Senator Carver's daughter?" the officer asked.

"Yes."

He didn't say another word, but drove faster. They rode in silence for half an hour before the officer veered off the highway at Carver's exit, taking every corner too fast. He'd covered the rest of the distance in far less than forty-five minutes.

Mike jumped from the car almost before it stopped and rushed to the front line of agents. He flipped open his wallet as he approached. "Mike Dorsen. FBI. Chicago division." That was the last assignment he'd been on. "The woman you saw is my girlfriend. Tell me what we're facing."

"Dude, you look like shit," the agent who seemed to be in charge said.

"Didn't ask you how I look. How did Zola look?"

The guy straightened his spine and held out a hand. "Jeff Roland."

Mike took it, waiting for an answer.

Roland sighed. "She wasn't in good shape. I'm sorry. They brought her here in the trunk of that car over there." He pointed to the silver vehicle that had been tailing them on the highway. "Duct tape everywhere. Her wrists behind her back. Her ankles. Knees. Face."

Mike fought the urge to punch the nearest...anything. "But you're sure she was alive?"

"Yes. She was fighting with everything she had."

Mike blew out a breath. Now that he knew what he was facing and where Zola was, he just needed to get her back. "Gonna need a gun," he told Roland.

ZOLA LAY ON the couch in her father's den still completely bound and gagged. She couldn't move a muscle except to pull her knees up closer. Her hands were numb. It was growing increasingly difficult to wiggle her fingers.

Her father was bound to a chair in the middle of the room facing her. His expression showed a constant fear and worry. His mouth was not covered, but every time he tried to reason with their captors, he was slapped.

"Listen," he tried again, "what do you want? I have the power to make it happen."

She wasn't sure he had the power to do anything of the sort, but she knew he had to speak the words over and over in an attempt to reason with the four men who rarely acknowledged them and infrequently used English.

It was growing dark outside which meant she had been there for a few hours, and her circulation had been impaired even longer. She relaxed her shoulders again so her hands wouldn't hurt so badly. It didn't work.

Her father's face was swollen on both sides, his eyes half-closed from being punched several times before she arrived. She imagined she looked even worse, but he might not know she'd been in a car accident.

He licked his lips and spoke again. "Would you like me to talk to the police? See if I can get you what you want?"

They were hostages. Pawns. In what game?

One of the men marched across the room, grabbed her father by the chin, and growled into his face. "What I want is for you to keep your fucking mouth shut." He whipped her father's face to one side, almost causing the chair to topple over.

It wobbled and then righted itself.

A booming voice penetrated the house through a megaphone outside for the fourth or fifth time. "You are surrounded. We can't negotiate with you if we don't know what your terms are. Please send someone out or allow us to send someone in to discuss what we can do to end this peacefully."

If Zola could have laughed—and if this had been a movie instead of her real life—she would have. Negotiate? Peacefully? That was never going to happen.

Three of the men huddled in the corner talking in soft voices while one stood guard at the window, a machine gun in his hand. He waved it around so flippantly she feared they would all accidentally be shot.

Finally, the men broke apart. One spoke to the man on guard, and one left the room.

At least something was happening. The standoff was worse than being beaten or tossed around in many ways.

Where was Mike? She concentrated hard to keep from letting tears fall because her nose would run and make it difficult to breathe.

Had he survived the crash? She could only hope he was either in the hospital or right outside freaking the fuck out. The last possibility made her both hopeful and afraid. If he was out there somewhere, he was livid beyond belief. And scared.

The front door opened and slammed shut. Voices

filtered from the entryway to the library. English. They had finally let someone inside. She couldn't hear specific words, but her father's head was cocked to one side in concentration.

Minutes passed. The front door opened and slammed shut again. The man who had gone to the door returned, stomping angry, yelling at his three comrades in heated Arabic. He pointed at Zola several times and her father.

Would they be killed? It seemed probable. These men were trapped. No way would they let the hostages go. If they were going down, they would likely take Zola and her father out first.

Deep breaths in and out through her nose. *Stay calm. You need to remain sharp.* Though she had no idea what good that would do her since she would never be able to stand upright, let alone fight.

The man who seemed to be the ringleader ran a hand through his hair and then stared out the window in silence again.

She had no idea who these guys were. They obviously weren't the Johanssons. She'd seen pictures of that family. They were Caucasian. But there had to be a connection.

After several tense moments of pacing, the man at the window pulled a piece of paper from his back pocket and shook it to unfold it. He strode over to her father and held it up. "Perhaps you can reason with your American friends out there. These are the terms. If they don't meet them all, you and your daughter die."

Her father nodded vigorously. "I'll talk to them."

The man leaned forward, getting in her father's face.

"Tonight. They have two hours. Every man on this list has to call in and let me know they are free or I shoot your daughter first and then you. We clear?" His English was almost perfect. If he wasn't American, he had at least been in the country for a long time.

"Understood."

The man pulled out a cell phone and dialed a number. He put the call on speaker while it rang and held it up to her father's ear. He shook the paper out again, righting it in front of her father's face.

Someone answered. "Assad? I'm glad you called. Can we discuss your terms?"

Her father licked his lips. "This is Senator Carver."

The man named Assad didn't say a word. In fact, his lips were pursed. He pointed at the paper.

The agent on the phone spoke again. "Senator Carver. Are you injured?"

"No. I'm fine. I'm going to read you a list of people who need to be released from prison. You have two hours to make this happen or these men will kill us." Her father was shaking as he spoke. She'd never in her life seen him rattled. He was so nervous, his voice cracked. Of course, she'd also never seen him held as a hostage by four madmen.

"Assad," the agent said, addressing the darker man instead of her father, "I will do everything in my power to make that happen, but it takes time to get people released from prison. I might not be able to do it in two hours. As a show of good faith, I'll get as many as possible as quick as possible, but then I need you to also extend the courtesy of giving me more time."

Assad shook his head vehemently toward her father. Zola had no idea why he didn't just speak for himself.

"That won't be possible," her father continued. "His terms are firm."

"We'll do our best." The agent sounded deflated.

Her father read off the names slowly. The list was long. Over a dozen people. Several of the names she recognized. Either her office or another had put most of them away for life. Among those names was Johansson, the mall shooter whose parents had been suspected of terrorizing Zola for the last weeks.

When he finished reading the list, Assad yanked the phone away and disconnected, putting it in his back pocket.

Zola's head was pounding. She was certain she had a concussion as well as a few lacerations. She didn't think she was bleeding from any open wound, but the tightness on her forehead in several spots indicated dried blood. When she tried to scrunch the skin above her eyes, it pulled tightly, stabbing pain piercing behind her eyes.

She flexed her fingers again. They were even more swollen and numb. They had stopped hurting though, which she took as a bad sign.

The room grew silent for a long time, the only sound that of the men pacing in front of the windows.

The house was large, and Zola tried to imagine why the SWAT team didn't break in through the back. But then again, if there was any sign or noise indicating a breach, she had no doubt she would be shot.

She closed her eyes, breathing evenly, gathering energy. She thought of Mike, imagining his smile, the way he kissed the sensitive spot behind her ear. The way he whispered words of love so faintly she could barely hear them. She pictured him doing that twelve years ago and again this week.

She didn't want to die here today. She wanted to live to spend the next seventy years with him like he suggested. Why had she dug her feet in so hard, insisting she couldn't and wouldn't quit her job for him? It seemed so petty all of the sudden. She would do anything for him. Go to the ends of the Earth. Walk through burning coals. Become a housewife.

If she could just get out of this mess alive.

What were the chances? She dragged old hostage cases out of the recesses of her mind. She knew the statistics on hostages. Her chances were slim, especially since the terrorists holding her were Islamic extremists. She shook that dreary thought from her head. She was lucky she was alive still even now. And every man in the room had several weapons, most of them capable of mowing down half the street.

When the phone rang in Assad's back pocket, she flinched, opening her eyes to watch him take the call. He didn't speak. He simply listened. She imagined the agent in charge updating him.

Suddenly, he broke the silence. "No, you listen to me, you entitled white prick. You have fifty-three more minutes, and then I kill these two equally white smug members of your society who have worked tirelessly to put my people behind bars. You hear me? Every one of those people must call me in the next fifty-three minutes with good news or this senator and his daughter are dead." He hung up.

Zola held her breath. Nothing had changed. There was no reason to freak out. But as she grew closer to the time of her execution, her nerves increased. Fifty-three minutes. What if her life was going to end in fifty-three minutes?

She hadn't told Mike she loved him. She hadn't lived with him. She had so many firsts she wanted to experience with him. She wanted children. A home with a fence. More time…

The phone rang again. Assad answered it without a word. He listened for several seconds and then hung up. "That's one. Thirteen more to go," he told the room at large.

As the next half hour went by, Zola tried to keep track of the number of calls, assuming all of them were another freed criminal. She cringed knowing that these were murderers. Each of them had undoubtedly killed many people in the name of a warped version of their religion.

She didn't feel her life was equal to the release of so many criminals. For one thing, each of them would then kill again. If the man in charge outside was smart, he would let Zola and her father die rather than release so many horrific individuals. This was an obvious case where the hostages needed to be sacrificed. If she could tell him that, she would. But she would never have the chance.

Another part of her, a selfish part, wanted them to all be freed so she would live. However, her rational mind told her she was not going to live in either scenario. These men didn't even have masks. She could ID them all in a heartbeat. No way were they going to let her or her father live.

Two more calls came in. What were they up to? Eight?

One of the men grabbed a black backpack she hadn't noticed from the corner of the room and lugged it to the center, setting it on the coffee table. Judging by the flex of his muscles under the black T-shirt he wore, and the strain on his face, the bag was heavy.

He unzipped it and carefully removed a canister. After setting it on the table, he pulled something else small out of the backpack and tossed it aside.

A bomb?

Dammit.

She widened her gaze, glancing at her father to see sweat running down his face in shear panic.

The man leaned over the device, attaching several wires to set it up and then pushing a button on the front that caused a ticking noise to fill the room.

"There," he declared. He spun around, holding up a black square that looked a bit like a pager from two decades ago. With a wicked grin on his face, he approached Zola.

She nearly peed herself contemplating his intent. He roughly rolled her forward, opened her stiff, swollen fingers, and pressed the box into her palm. "You better squeeze that tight, girl. If you let go of the button on the side, we all die. You hear me?"

She stopped breathing, all her concentration going to the fucking box in her hand. Her fingers were so numb she had no way of feeling the box beyond the fact that it was touching her. She didn't know if there was really a button on the side or not. He could have been fucking with her mind.

Or she might hold the power to blow up the house, taking out all four men, herself, and her father.

Fuck.

The responsibility was too much. Should she let it go and save countless other lives who would be lost in future mass shootings or bombings at the hands of the fourteen terrorists being released from prison as she lay on the couch being used as a pawn?

"If your people try anything stupid out there, I shoot you, you die. It will take a few seconds for your hand to unfurl, giving me and my men plenty of time to escape before the gas is released from the canister. You and your father will count the seconds until you both die. It will be painful."

Zola froze. Not a bomb. Biological warfare. The horror of the situation closed in on her, threatening to cause her to black out. They would die immediately if she did. And she wasn't ready to make that choice yet.

Rationally, it wouldn't be just the men being released from prison who would be stopped, but also the four in the room. She held too much power. If she somehow lived through this, she would have to live with the guilt of her decision for the rest of her life.

She knew she would be a victim either way. These men were angry at her for prosecuting their terrorist friends and her father for getting easier laws passed that made it possible for her to convict. No way did they intend to let Zola and her father live.

Another call came in. Nine?

She held the black box as tightly as possible with limited use of her fingers. Every ounce of her concentration went to her grip. If she moved even an inch to alleviate some of the discomfort in her shoulders, she would lose her grip.

Another call. She lost track of how many that was.

Chapter Fifteen

WHILE HE WAITED for a weapon, Mike ran his hands through his hair so many times it was a wonder there was any left. He wished he had one of his own guns from the back of the rental car, but even the one he'd had tucked into his waist had freed itself during the accident. He had nothing.

Finally Jeff Roland set a Glock in his palm. "You're not in charge here, Dorsen."

"With all due respect, your girlfriend and her father aren't inside that house." He examined the chamber and palmed the weapon.

"This is a hostage situation. We have protocol to follow."

"Yep. I'm aware. I've been through situations you can't even begin to imagine"—he lifted his head to face Roland—"sir."

"This isn't a contest. Don't posture with me. I'm not in the mood."

"And I'm not in the mood to lose the love of my life

today, either. So, let's work together to ensure we both get what we want." He met Roland's gaze again. "Get me a wire. I want to know everything that's going on."

"Fucking SEALs," Roland muttered under his breath.

If Mike had been in any other frame of mind, he would have grinned.

Five minutes later, he had a mic and an earpiece. "So, here's the deal."

"Why do I suspect I'm not going to like this?"

"Don't care if you do like it. We're doing it anyway." Mike pointed to the corner of the house. "See that trellis over there?"

Roland groaned. "You have got to be fucking kidding me. This isn't some horror movie. We're in the middle of a hostage situation."

"One in which the good guy happens to have used that trellis twelve years ago after climbing out of the bedroom window so that a sexy teenage girl's father wouldn't know she had a gentleman suitor in the house after curfew."

Roland groaned, rubbing a hand down his face. "Let me repeat myself, you have got to be fucking kidding me."

"Nope."

"And what makes you think the window is unlocked and not hooked up to the alarm system? That was a damn long time ago."

"Because I removed the sensor on that window myself. Both pieces. Stuck them together and attached them to the inside of the sill so that they were always connected even when the window was open. I also broke the lock."

Roland stared at him. "You were one randy teenager."

"Yeah, don't get too excited. She wasn't that kind of girl. But it didn't keep me from spending every moment I could with her. I knew I had a good thing the moment I saw her." He rushed on, "Now I'm going to get inside the house and survey what we're up against. You're going to keep me informed from out here. And on my call, your men need to shoot to kill."

"I hate this plan."

"You have a better one?"

"No." Roland sighed loudly, his shoulders slumping. "Don't make me regret this. It's so far out of protocol, my ass is liable to get fired even if you succeed."

"I'll take the heat and cover your ass, Roland. You just keep me informed."

"Fine." Roland turned around as if not watching would somehow exonerate him of all blame.

Mike ignored the throbbing pain in his head as he rushed around the side of the house. It was dusk. He was protected partially by the growing darkness. In addition, few people had their attention focused on the side of the house.

He prayed to God everything he told Roland was true—that the window was indeed still unlocked and the sensor still misplaced. And for the love of all that was holy, that damn trellis needed to hold his older, heavier body up after twelve additional years of wear and tear.

He held his breath as he climbed the side of the house and then crept across the slightly slanted roof to get to the window hidden around the side in the near darkness.

His eyes were swollen, leaving his vision impaired. The

laceration on his forehead had been closed with a butterfly bandage. He was banged up and bruised over every inch of his body. And his knee was screaming in pain.

But none of that mattered, and his adrenaline was pumping so hard he hated to consider how much worse he would feel when this was over.

He hesitated only a second when he set his fingers under the edge of the window. "Please, God." And then he eased the window open, an internal smile all he could muster.

Ten seconds later, he was in the room. It was no longer Zola's room, but a guest room. Everything had been redone, but somehow no one had noticed the rigged window after all these years.

The lights weren't on, of course, but he could see well enough to make his way across the floor to the open doorway. "I'm in," he whispered into the mic. "I'll give you a layout as soon as I can, and then you mobilize."

"You are one crazy bastard, Dorsen."

SILENCE. PACING. STARING out the window.

Zola watched the man who had set up the canister. His smug face would haunt her for the rest of her fifteen minutes on earth. He was the man responsible for watching. And he turned around again, stared at Zola with a crazed look in his eye, and leaned against the window sill.

Two seconds later, all hell broke loose. The room filled with gunfire.

She watched in horror as the man looking at her fell to

the floor, a shot through the back of his head most likely.

The man called Assad hit the floor next, his body slumping dramatically forward, blood running from his forehead.

The last two men rushed into the center of the room, guns drawn.

Zola had no idea why they didn't shoot her or her father. Perhaps because they were busy trying to figure out where the gunfire was coming from and remain alive.

They didn't have a chance, however. Several more shots rang out, missing their target. Amid the chaos, a hand landed on Zola's shoulder. She flinched, fear making her almost drop the device in her palm. Her eyes widened as she tipped her face to the side.

Mike. He leaned around her without looking at her, and made two final shots to the men in the center of the room. Instantly, they were down. Not moving.

She had never been so happy to see anyone in her life, but she needed to remember the damn button she gripped.

"Mike," her father shouted as several members of SWAT filled the room, "the canister. Zola has the controller in her hands."

"Fuck." Mike leaned over her, carefully tipping her body forward. He touched her fingers, though she could hardly feel them. "Baby, I need you to let go."

She shook her head, trying to speak through the tape.

He held both her hands securely with one of his and reached with his other hand to ease the tape off her mouth.

She rushed to explain. "Button," she gasped. "I'm holding it down."

"Okay, babe. I'm going to take it over for you." He spun his head around. "Get everyone out of here. Now. Get her father out. All of you out," he commanded.

Her father was frantically pleading with anyone who would listen, but Zola only looked at Mike's face, tuning everyone else out. "You came."

He smiled. "I'm here. We're going to get you out of here. Hang on one more minute."

Someone leaned over the back of the couch, their shadow darkening the area. "Dorsen, let the bomb squad handle this. You get out."

"Not a fucking chance in hell. I'm doing it, or nobody is doing it. Get everyone out. Let me free Zola, then you can send the bomb squad in. And let them know it's not a bomb. It's a biological weapon." Thank God he recognized it with a glance. He would realize this was no bomb.

She squeezed her hands inside his larger one. He had her though. She wasn't going to let go with his fingers so tight around hers.

He cupped her face with his free hand. "Zola, look at me. You're okay. We're going to get you out of here."

She nodded, licking her parched lips. Her face hurt. Everything hurt. "My wrists," she whispered.

"I know. Can't release them yet. The rush of blood to your fingers would be dangerous."

Someone cut her legs free, however. Her feet were sore but not nearly as compromised as her hands. He was right. Removing the tape would be a bad idea. "It hurts," she told him, leaning her forehead forward to set it against his chin.

"I know, baby. We're going to fix it in just a few seconds." He tipped her head back and glanced around again. "What the fuck are you all waiting for? Get out. Fast. She can't hold on much longer."

People rushed around. Her father leaned over her. "Zola."

She met his pained gaze. "It'll be okay, Dad."

"I love you." He set a hand on Mike's shoulder.

"I love you too, Dad," she managed to say without bursting into tears.

He turned his gaze to Mike. "Get her out alive, son."

"I will, sir. You have my word."

Someone grabbed her father by both arms and pulled him away. "I'm sorry, Senator, but we need to get you a safe distance away."

When he was gone, she set her gaze on Mike's. "I love you," she whispered, her voice choked.

"Don't." He shook his head. "Don't act like you aren't going to live. We're in this together now. I'm right here. You hold on. If you go, I go. And I don't intend for this to be my last day on earth, so you have no choice."

Someone shouted from the doorway. "Okay, Dorsen. Room's clear. House's clear. Send Zola out when you have the remote free, and we'll get the bomb squad in here ASAP."

Silence.

Deafening silence.

Tears ran down her face. She was more scared now than she had been for the last several hours. "Mike…"

He cupped her face one more time and kissed her soundly. "I'm going to figure out where the button is and then ease my finger over it. When I tell you to let go, you release the box and run. You hear me?"

She shook her head, sobbing. "Not leaving you here."

"Yes. You are. I'll be right behind you. It will be much easier for me to pass it off to the bomb squad. We will get it dismantled. Neither of us is going to die today."

"Promise me."

"Zola, baby, I swear."

Fear gripped her, but she had no other options. She nodded. "Okay, do it."

He released her face after another quick kiss and leaned over her back, rolling her gently forward onto her belly. "I see the button. It's pressed to your palm. I'm going to ease my thumb against your hand and transfer the pressure from you to me."

"Okay." She could feel almost nothing. All she heard for several moments was the beat of her heart ringing in her ears.

"I've got it. Zola, I'm in control of it now. You can let go."

She couldn't though. She couldn't release the grip. Her fingers were swollen and not obeying any commands as if frostbitten. "I can't, Mike. I can't."

He pried her fingers open with his other hand. Finally she was free, and he stood, backing away from her, the controller in his hand. "Run, baby."

She worked hard to pull herself to sitting with her arms still useless and her legs barely working themselves. And then she rocked forward to propel herself to standing. She wanted to say so many things, but Mike's face was hard.

"Zola, run."

She turned and rushed from the room as fast as she could, knowing he needed her to get out so the bomb squad could get in. It would be okay. *He* would be okay. He had to be. There was no other option.

Zola rushed out the front door, barely clearing the frame before two members of the bomb squad ran in around her without a word.

She kept moving forward, but was quickly met by an agent, who hustled her farther away from the house and immediately cut the tape from her wrists.

She winced at the incredible pain.

The man released her arms, and she drew them around to her front slowly, her shoulders screaming. Her hands felt like they were being stabbed with a million tiny needles.

Her father was by her side a moment later. "Zola. Oh God. Are you okay?" He reached for her as she tried to rub her palms together to get the circulation moving.

A medic crowded in beside her next. "Let me see, ma'am." He wrapped a hand gently around her arm. "Let's move into the light so I can check your injuries."

She nodded, biting her lip, unable to speak through the pain. A tear ran down her face.

The paramedic spoke again when they reached the open doors of his ambulance. The light spilled around them. "Rub your palms together gently to get the blood flowing. I know it hurts, but that's a good sign. And they're still red. The stabbing will stop in a few minutes."

She hoped so. All she could do was nod and try to get them to function. She wiggled her fingers.

Her dad stood silently at her side.

She glanced back at the house. "Why isn't Mike out yet?"

"I don't know, honey. They're working on it. He probably knows more about biological warfare than anyone on the scene. They need his help."

"He promised," she stated unnecessarily.

Her father set a hand on her shoulder. "I know. And he won't break that promise. He'll be here."

She stared at her dad. *Like the last time he made me a promise? And you forced him to break it?*

Obviously realizing where her thoughts had gone, he sighed. "I was a fool, Zola. I'm so sorry. I totally messed with your life. I had no business interfering."

She said nothing. She had to forgive him. She would forgive him. He was her father. But it would take time.

"Ma'am, we need to get you in the ambulance. You need medical care."

She lifted her gaze to the paramedic. "I'm not going anywhere yet. Don't even suggest it."

The guy glanced at the house and nodded. He was tall and lanky with brown hair that hung over his forehead. In a different life—one in which the only man she'd ever loved didn't exist—she would have been attracted to him.

She flexed her fingers, the pain dulling to something more manageable.

"I'm sorry you got dragged into this, honey. I never would've been able to forgive myself if anything had happened to you."

She kept her gaze on the front of the house while she

spoke to her father. "I don't understand how they found me. We changed cars. We stayed low. How the hell did they manage to track me down and run us off the highway?"

"GPS locator on your key fob." He sighed. "It was probably in your purse."

"What?" She glanced at her father.

He nodded, cringing. "They took my phone, scrolled through the aps, and realized my phone had the ability to track you."

She groaned. "Right. Shit." The fob had been in her purse forever. It had never occurred to her for a moment that she could be responsible for giving away their location.

A commotion behind her had her spinning around to face the house.

Mike stepped outside as several people cheered. And then he scanned the area. The moment he spotted her, he raced across the lawn toward the ambulance.

Seconds later, she was in his arms, her hands hanging limp at her sides as she tried not to touch anything. They were still tingling as if they'd been asleep.

He held her tight and then leaned back to look her over. "Jesus, babe, you look like shit."

She smiled. "So do you."

"Let's get you to the hospital."

"Mike, the last time I saw you I wasn't sure you were even alive. So I know you have injuries I can't even see."

"Maybe a few." He smiled back.

Her father cleared his throat.

They both turned to face him. She would be angry for

a long time, but for now she needed to be glad they were all alive.

He looked at Mike. "Thank you. There aren't enough words to express my gratitude. You saved my daughter's life, and I owe you mine too." He swallowed. "And I also need to apologize again for my actions when you were younger. I was wrong. I hope someday you can both forgive me."

Zola didn't have words, but she did lean forward and kiss his cheek. "I'll call you tomorrow, Dad."

He gave a wan smile and stepped back. "Get in the ambulance. You both look like you were in an accident."

Chapter Sixteen

One week later...

"YOU SURE YOU want to do this?" Mike asked Zola, eyeing her cautiously. She'd spent two nights in the hospital and then five nights at her father's house under strict orders to rest.

Mike had also spent two nights in the hospital under the careful eye of the doctors. Both of them had suffered a concussion in the car crash. Unbelievably, neither of them had any broken bones. Cuts and scrapes. A few stitches to her forehead. A few butterflies to his hairline.

But they were in one piece and recuperating.

After their release, Mike had needed to take care of several things to wrap up the case with the CIA. Lambert had asked him to take another case, half teasingly, and Mike had told him where he could shove that idea, also half teasingly. After five nights sleeping without Zola in his bed, he had made his way to her father's house and spent the next two nights lying next to her on top of the covers.

He wasn't about to stress his tenuous relationship with

her father any further than it already was by shoving their relationship in his face, but he also wasn't going to sleep in another room where he couldn't reach out every hour or so and make sure she was still real.

Mike had been surprised either Zola or her father had wanted to go back to the house at all. But they'd insisted. Finally, he and Zola had returned to Norfolk. Mike, for one, was glad he didn't have to spend another day in the noisy environment where workers were doing repairs from the shootout in the den. The hammering alone had given him a constant headache.

Now they were back in Norfolk, and he was unlocking the front door of Tex's house. He had it rented for another two weeks.

"Why wouldn't I want to stay here? It's gorgeous. The view is amazing. The inside is cozy. It couldn't be any safer unless you posted guards outside. Plus, all the bad guys have been captured or killed, remember?" Even the released terrorists had been brought back into custody. None of them had ever been out of sight of the members of SWAT tracking them until they could be re-apprehended in the first place.

He shot her a glance as he turned the lock. He didn't bother pointing out that the world was filled with bad guys, many of whom were still alive and well, some of whom were probably equally pissed with his feisty woman who put them in jail.

Instead, he pointed out the other obvious elephant. "It doesn't bother you that two men were lurking around this place while we were luckily out to dinner?"

"Nope." She passed under his arm as he swung the door open.

A moment later, he shut the door and reset the alarm.

"Everything is right where we left it."

"I hope so," he teased. "If it isn't, we aren't staying here tonight."

She wrapped an arm around him and giggled. "I've missed you."

He lifted a brow as he brushed her soft hair off her forehead, trying not to wince at the angry scar where the stitches had been removed yesterday. "I haven't been out of your sight for two days. How could you miss me?"

She giggled again. "I wanted to see more of you."

"More than every second except when you showered and used the bathroom?" He knew what she was telling him, but he still enjoyed the banter.

She rolled her eyes. "Yes, I'd rather you be in the shower with me and wear far less clothing during the day and none at night."

He pulled her closer, finding it hard to keep his hands off her if only to remind himself regularly she was still alive. "I think those things can all be arranged."

"You don't have to go back to work for two more weeks, right?"

"Nope."

"And since I'm taking two weeks also, I say we make the most out of it. It has to last us awhile. Who knows where you'll be sent or for how long."

He wasn't convinced this idea of the two of them going about their lives as normal was a good one, but until they came up with a better plan, they were stuck. She had mentioned bargaining with God during her hours of terror, but he argued that in the light of day she wasn't cut out to waddle around barefoot and pregnant, baking cookies and making casseroles.

Within months she would regret the decision and it would eat at her until it came between them.

For the next two weeks, they had agreed to table the discussion and get to know each other all over again.

The first thing Mike wanted to do was peel off her clothes while backing her down the hall until they fell into bed. He intended to explore every inch of her, fulfilling every image he'd conjured in his mind for the last week.

It was probably for the best that she'd chosen to stay with her dad. If she'd gone back to her own condo, Mike probably wouldn't have been able to keep his hands to himself, and she'd needed to recuperate.

He didn't have the patience to head for the bedroom yet though. Instead, still standing inside the front door, he reached beneath her sweater and flattened his hands on her bare skin, making her shudder. "Ms. Carver, this shirt has got to go," he stated as he shoved it up over her head and dropped it on the floor.

"Mr. Dorsen, tit for tat, I agree." She grabbed the hem of his polo and dragged it over his head too, lifting onto tiptoes while he bent at the knees to help her.

"Ms. *Carver*," he stated, unable to control his shock when he lowered his gaze to her tits. "Wherever did you get something so scandalous?" He cupped her breasts through the black lacy lingerie that barely covered her nipples and left miles of creamy flesh around the edges.

For a moment he couldn't breathe. She was so stunning.

"You like?"

"God, Zola. You have to ask?" He thumbed both her nipples through the material, forcing a whimper from her lips.

"I guess that's a yes," she whispered breathily.

"Please tell me there's a super skimpy swatch of lace that matches this excuse for a bra under your jeans."

"You'll have to take them off to find out," she teased.

He slowly backed her up until her ass hit the wall next to the front door, and then he lowered to a crouch—ignoring the twitch in his knee—and popped the button on her jeans. When he slid the zipper down and then tugged the denim over her hips, his breath caught. "You naughty girl."

She moaned, flattening her palms on the wall at her sides.

The matching item she wore under those jeans was not a pair of panties at all. It was a thong. And that was also a stretch. But that wasn't the only thing that caught his eye. "You're a super naughty girl." He leaned forward, reverently inhaling her musk, unable to take his gaze off the small strip of well-groomed strawberry-blond hair that peeked out the top of the thong.

He didn't take his eyes off her as he finished removing her jeans. He had to tap her feet to get her to kick her heels off, but when she did, he steadied her with a hand at her hip while she stepped out of the jeans.

"Zola…" His voice caught in his throat. He couldn't decide if he wanted to stare at her in this thong that held only the tiniest of surprises behind it or if he wanted to yank it off her body to finish the visual in his head of what lay behind the triangle.

He decided on the first option for the time being and pressed a soft kiss to the lace before licking a line around the edge of the thong while she gasped and grabbed his shoulders to steady herself.

When she lifted onto her toes once again, he took advantage of the extra few inches and dragged his tongue over her pussy, reaching between her legs to hit her folds.

She moaned, already so ready for him he could taste it. "We didn't make it to the bedroom," she mumbled.

"Overrated." He grabbed her hips, held her steady, and sucked her clit into his mouth through the thong.

She squealed, pressing her pussy against him wantonly.

He eased his hands around until he could reach under the elastic with his thumbs, pulling the lace away from her pussy. When the air hit her, she gasped.

He reached under the material and stroked her folds with his tongue.

"Mike…" Her voice was distant, though he wasn't sure if it was because she was so gone she had whispered or if he was so horny, his ears were ringing.

Either way he was lost to her. "I need to taste you, baby."

"You have tasted me. Nothing has changed. Take your jeans off and make love to me." She hesitated, and then added, "Please."

Instead of heeding her advice, he eased her thong down her legs and pushed them wider. When he leaned forward to set his knees on the floor, his injured knee complained, but he adjusted his weight and focused on the feast before him.

Starting slow, to keep her on the edge, he stroked his thumbs over her lower lips and parted them.

She gasped when he pushed both thumbs an inch inside her, stretching her open. Her legs trembled, which made him even hornier. His cock was pressed uncomfortably tight in his jeans, but he didn't want to stop enjoying her to adjust or take off his jeans yet.

When he set his mouth over her bare clit and sucked it between his lips, she rose onto her tiptoes, buried her fingers in his hair, and moaned.

He couldn't tell if she was pushing on his head or trying to pull him closer, but he liked it. The sting of her fingers against his scalp caused his cock to stiffen further.

He flicked his tongue over her clit rapidly while her noises increased, the sounds rising and falling as he imagined her head rocking back and forth against the wall.

When she froze, her thighs going rigid against his shoulders, he flattened his tongue over her clit and inhaled long and slow while she came.

He held her close, keeping the intense pressure against her clit and inside her as she rode out the waves. It wasn't until she lowered onto her flat feet and sighed that he eased out of her pussy and released her clit.

"Mike…" Sultry, sated, fulfilled.

He wiped his lips on his hand and rose in front of her,

sliding his body along hers as he did. When he was fully standing, she tipped her head back, a languid, satisfied smile filling her entire expression.

She set her lips on his ear, mimicking the way he normally did hers. In a soft, sultry voice she whispered, "I don't think you heard me."

"What, baby?" he asked.

"Take your jeans off. Now."

He grinned, but his hands went to his button, and then his zipper, and then he was shoving the denim down his thighs until the jeans fell to the floor. He kicked off his shoes and then his jeans while his lips found hers. He licked the seam of her mouth first, but when she let him in, he plunged, tasting every inch of her while sharing the flavor of her pussy.

If it squicked her out, he would never know. She faked it well, consuming him with as much desire as he did her.

She broke the kiss first, nibbling on his lips. "Now, Mike. I'm dying here."

He grabbed her waist and lifted her off the floor, dragging her against the wall and holding her up under her arms. When she was high enough, he lodged his cock at her entrance and slowly lowered her over the tip.

He forced himself to watch her face, taking in every nuance as her eyes fluttered and then clouded and then closed. Her face was flushed a deep shade of red he loved on her. It made him increase his pace, knowing she was as aroused as him. Maybe more so.

He was close. So close. But he wanted to watch her come again first, so he kept his gaze on her and forced himself to ignore the driving need to come.

Her mouth fell open, her lips swollen and wet from their kiss. God, she was fucking gorgeous.

He gritted his teeth as he continued to lift her off him and then plunged back into her tight warmth. Just when he thought there was no way in hell he could hold off another second, she came. Her head slumped forward over his shoulder as she moaned louder and then repeated his name over and over. "Mike... Mike, Mike, Mike..."

He emptied himself inside her, holding her tight over his cock buried deep. His pulsing matched hers beat for beat.

Emotion swept through him. Damn, he loved her. Was it too soon to tell her? She told him as much before running from her father's house a week ago, but that had been in an extremely stressful situation. Would she say it again now?

ZOLA HAD NEVER been so happy in her life. Three blissful days of nothing but lounging around on the beach with the man she had loved for almost half her life. It was insane how things worked out. Their relationship was both new and old at the same time.

Everything they did in bed or even getting to know each other was fresh and fun, but on the flip side they fell into a comfortable pace that was no different from when they were teenagers. At heart, they had not changed. Their passion for their work and each other was the same. They each had fire and drive that most people they knew didn't have.

In some couples that sameness would have been too much. Perhaps driven them apart. But not Zola and Mike. They thrived off talking over one another and falling in love all over again.

Ignoring their real lives and the jobs they had put on hold for two weeks, they spent most of their time naked in bed or wrapped up in coats on the beach where the temperature outside was frigid most days. Gorgeous but cold.

She giggled as she gripped his hand and dragged him farther down to the edge of the water. It was early in the morning. Most people weren't out yet, and it wasn't tourist season, so locals weren't inclined to endure this cold.

He groaned. "How far are we going? I like you better inside the house. You wear too many layers when we come out here."

She laughed again. "Get a grip, big guy. We're getting some exercise. It's called walking. It's a half hour out of your day. The sun is warm. The waves are beautiful. The sand feels good beneath my tennis shoes. Lifting weights and running indoors on a treadmill aren't the only forms of exercise on the planet."

"I think I'm more inclined to go with your initial assessment the first day you arrived."

"What was that?" She cocked her head to one side, her brow furrowed.

"You couldn't figure out why someone would want to vacation on a cold beach at the wrong time of year."

She rolled her eyes. "I get it now. I'm hooked. We get

the best of both worlds. Days outside in the fresh air where we're wearing too many clothes to be tempted, and nights inside naked where we're wearing too few clothes to care about the beach. If it were summer, we wouldn't even spend five minutes out here. One look at you in your trunks and I'd be hauling your ass back inside."

His smile was infectious. And then he reared back and laughed. "That's so complicated, I'm not even sure I followed your logic. But"—he enveloped her in his arms—"I do know I'm ready to go back into the house and switch to the naked part." He kissed her soundly, sending a shudder down her body.

Every time his lips or hand or any part of him touched her, she nearly swooned. Her knees grew week. Her nipples pebbled. Her pussy moistened, preparing itself to take him. Which she would gladly do anywhere any time.

She was a new woman. Totally enamored. Her first real vacation in years, and definitely the first time she was with a man she really enjoyed and wanted to give herself to completely. Not just her body, but her soul.

So, what was the problem?

Niggling in the back of her mind was the fact that they had two separate lives. They were on the vacation of a lifetime, but it had to end. In eleven days, they would have to return to their real lives. Lives that didn't mesh. Lives that were intense and happened in different states.

Sure, in the heat of things while she was being held hostage by madmen, she'd promised God she would gladly quit her job and become a housewife to a man who would take his next assignment God only knew where. However, in the light of day, she knew that would suffocate her.

It would kill her to leave her passion.

It would kill him to quit his work with the FBI.

Vacation was amazing. But life would creep back in to take over, and then what?

"Enough air," he said. "Let's go back inside." He grabbed her hand and tugged.

She shook off the melancholy and followed him. His ass… Damn… Even in jeans it was fine. But naked… The thought of getting those jeans off him again…

She shuddered as he dragged her down the edge of the water back toward the house he had rented. She hoped one day she would get to meet the man he spoke to often. Tex. John Keegan. Obviously, they were close, even though Mike had never met the man in person either.

As they burst through the back door, laughing and peeling off layers, Mike's cell phone rang in his pocket.

He pulled it out and took the call, his face still pink from the cold air and smiling broadly from their banter and the excitement of their next inevitable activity.

She tore off her gloves and dropped them on the table, turning to face him.

His expression had switched in a heartbeat, going from warm and happy to grim and concerned. His brow furrowed, and his lips fell. "Tex. Slow down. What the hell?"

She stopped removing layers and wrapped her arms around his middle, tipping her face up to meet his gaze. Her heart beat faster. Adrenaline replaced arousal.

"You have got to be kidding me." He rubbed his forehead, refusing to meet her gaze.

That was the worst part of all. His eyes wandered around the room, never landing on hers. Though his arm snaked around her to hold her close, he still didn't look at her.

"Right... Yes... Okay... Fuck... No... Motherfucking... Okay." On that last word, his voice dropped and he set the phone on the counter behind him.

For long moments, she waited, no sound in the room except their breathing. In. Out. In. Out. Loud. In sync.

She knew as soon as one of them spoke, the world as they knew it was over.

Finally, Mike inhaled deeply, blew out the breath even longer, and lowered his gaze to hers. "Fucking Johanssons are still after you."

"What?" she screamed.

He lowered his face to hers, grabbed her chin, and held her so that she had to look at him. "We'll get these assholes. I swear, if it's the last thing I do, I will make you safe."

"But why? I thought..." Her mind wandered through so many thoughts. Weren't the Johanssons in cahoots with the four men who took her and her father hostage? They were all dead. The Johanssons had been taken in for questioning. It had been so obvious to Zola, and to Mike, that they were guilty of conspiring to get revenge. Surely they were behind bars?

"They were released last night. Apparently my contact at the CIA either didn't know or failed to fill us in, but they got out on bond and are back at home as if they had never been arrested."

"You're shitting me?" How was that possible? Who the fuck was on that case? If she had been the attorney assigned to those idiots…

"I wish I was. But no. And Tex just happened to catch wind of their movement."

"How?" she interrupted.

Mike grinned. "Tex is a genius. With a computer, he is a God. He had their movement flagged and knew before any of us they were out on bond and wreaking havoc once again."

"And he thinks I'm in danger?" She fought the chill, holding Mike tighter.

"Worse than that. He *knows* you're in danger. He watched every message they sent since their release and every communication they've had. The group of terrorists who held you hostage at your father's house weren't nearly as closely involved with the Johanssons as we thought. They had bigger fish to fry. They wanted the release of multiple terrorists. Mohammad Johansson was just one of a long list of terrorists. But the Johanssons aren't satisfied since you haven't paid for your part in getting their son put away, so they hired someone else to finish the job. We need to get out of here. Now."

That was the last thing he said before a loud noise filled the air and her world flipped upside down.

Mike flattened her to the floor so fast he knocked the wind out of her. His body covered hers entirely. Her ears were ringing from the explosion. And the gorgeous sunny day was suddenly a cloud of darkness. Smoke filled the room.

Mike set his lips on her ear. "Don't make a sound. Stay low."

She couldn't have spoken if she wanted to. Or maybe that wasn't true. Maybe she would have started screaming, and that was what he was trying to avoid.

He eased himself to one side of her body, taking the pressure off while he reached with one hand to the small of his back where she knew he kept a gun.

She fought the need to cough in the smoke-filled room, covering her mouth with her hand. All she could think about was how much damage the house had endured. It wasn't their house. It belonged to Mike's good friend. And because of them, it was in shambles.

Rationally, she knew she should be more worried about her life and Mike's, but her mind shut that down in favor of concern for the destruction of property. Guilt ate at her.

Suddenly she realized Mike was talking to her. "Zola, babe. Zola?" He was whispering next to her ear, but urgently.

She yanked her eyes open and blinked at him.

"We need to move."

Move? Where? She couldn't focus. Her mind was scrambled.

He eased a hand under her lower back and tugged her up against him as he rose enough to lean her against the kitchen island, her butt on the floor, her feet stretched out in front of her. He cupped her chin. "Zola? Look at me."

She forced herself to focus on him, blinking. He was blurry. Or it was cloudy in the room. Or she was about to faint. Was there smoke? She didn't know what.

He spoke again, sounding far away. "Babe—" Gunfire cut him off.

Zola started to scream.

Mike slammed a hand over her mouth and leaned forward to cover her body with his more completely. He pushed her head down and twisted his body around, holding his gun up.

Drywall rained down around her, landing in her hair and all over their clothes.

"Come on." He grabbed her wrist and dashed across the kitchen in a crotched position, dragging her along behind him at a crawl.

At least no one was shooting at them for a few seconds. She had no idea what direction the shots had come from. When they reached the pantry, Mike opened the door slowly and ushered her inside.

Panic made her draw back, tugging on his wrist. "No," she insisted. The idea of being trapped inside a small closet seemed horrifying.

He ignored her, reached to the back of the pantry, and pulled open a small door she had never seen at ground level. "Safe room. Get inside. I'll lock it from out here. Don't open it for anyone. It's on a code. No one else can get in. Tex knows the code. Either I will open this door, or he will send someone else."

Her panic grew at the idea of separating from him. "No." She shook her head. "Unless you're coming in with me." How had she not known about the safe room?

He eased her smaller body closer, kissed her forehead, and then nudged her toward the entrance. "There's a door on the other side too. It leads to the master bedroom closet." He reached in and pulled something out. A flashlight. He handed it to her. "I'll be back as soon as I can."

She couldn't stop shaking her head. But it did no good. He all but pushed her through the entrance. With one last touch to her face, he met her gaze as she scrambled to turn around. "I love you." And then the door shut with a snick, cutting off almost all sound.

Panic like she'd never known set in as she turned on the flashlight and glanced around the room. She would have been impressed if the situation hadn't been so dire.

Tex's safe room was stocked with everything. It wasn't large, but it was big enough to stand up and wide enough for two people to lie on the air mattress she saw in the corner. Why did Tex have such an impressive safe room? Was he paranoid in general? Or did he have the sort of job that put him in danger? Probably the latter.

With a deep exhale, she turned off the light, leaned against the wall, set her chin on her drawn-up knees, and prayed to God Mike got them out of this situation and didn't get himself dead.

Chapter Seventeen

MIKE HAD NO idea what he was up against, but a huge weight lifted off him after he sequestered Zola in the safe room. At least he knew nothing would happen to her in there. Tex was thorough. Though Mike hadn't gone into the room or checked it out, Tex had told him it was there, and Mike had memorized the code. No one would get in there without knowing the six-digit code.

Another round of shots rang out, causing Mike to lower himself to the floor and crawl toward the back door. He needed to get out of the house before anything else. The longer he was inside, the more likely he would be backed into a corner. And he had no idea how many people were shooting at him.

What he also knew was that backup was on the way. Before he'd shoved Zola into the safe room, he had hit the panic button on the outside. Messages would have been sent to Tex and the authorities. Besides, Tex already knew the seriousness of the situation. He'd been the one to call with the warning moments before all hell broke loose.

Mike could have gotten into the safe room with Zola, and there was always the possibility he would regret the decision not to. But he wasn't the kind of man to cower and wait for someone to find him. Sequestering himself wasn't really his style.

He flattened himself to the kitchen wall next to the sliding glass doors and peered outside to see if there was movement.

Moments later the glass door shattered, and he rounded the corner to take advantage of the protection of the cabinets. Damn motherfuckers shooting up his friend's house. That in and of itself pissed him way the fuck off.

Another shot came from the back of the house. No one was on the patio, so he knew by the proximity they had to be hovering in the bushes off the deck.

He crawled to the front of the house, keeping low with his gun drawn. When he reached the front windows, he eased up the side and peeked out the edge.

Dammit. He could see booted feet under the bushes right off the porch. These fuckers were brazen. He was pissed, but they were no match for him. They had no idea what they were up against if they were stupid enough to think they could take out a former SEAL.

Maybe they didn't know he was a SEAL. There was a good chance of that. Perhaps they assumed Zola was just on the run with her boyfriend or a hired protector. In either case, they were in for a surprise. A one-way ticket to the third circle of hell.

The picture window had already been shot out, which gave him the ability to take a shot through the wide opening. In less than a few seconds, he rounded to face the fool who thought he was well-hidden, lined up the shot with the spot Mike assumed was the man's chest, and fired.

Bingo. The asshole fell forward through the bush and never moved another muscle. One down.

In response, several shots rang out from the back of the house.

Mike ducked back down to the floor and listened. He figured there were still two shooters in the back and no one currently in the front.

He crawled toward the kitchen again, praying Zola stayed in the safe room. If he had to worry about her at the same time, his job would be that much harder.

Silence reigned for several moments while he peered through the corner of the hole that had been the sliding glass doors and surveyed the situation. Indeed, there were two men out there, one at each corner of the deck. They were shuffling around more than they should. Amateur move. They were scared.

Good. That would make it easier to make them also dead.

Mike bided his time, watching, waiting, scoping. Finally, he rounded enough to take the easier shot, lined up, and took the farthest man out with a shot to the head.

Take that, motherfucker.

The man was dead so fast he didn't make a single sound. It took several more seconds before his comrade knew he was down.

Mike rolled his eyes as he ducked back around the corner.

A delayed onslaught of gunfire coming from one gun pelted the wall on the opposite side of the kitchen.

Mike glanced at the pantry. No movement. Good.

When silence reigned again, Mike waited a beat and then rose to take a glance out the window above the sink. No one. The guy had moved. Hopefully he retreated.

Where the fuck were the authorities? How long had it been? He stayed low as he made his way back to the front of the house, thinking the man may have rounded the house.

As soon as he rose to peer out the space where the picture window belonged, a noise behind him caught his attention. He spun around to find a man dressed in all black behind him, the barrel of his gun pointed directly at Mike.

Fuck.

"Not interested in you, asshole. Want the woman. Where is she?"

Mike eased around to face the man more fully. Five yards separated them. Who the hell was shooting outside? "What woman?"

The guy chuckled for half a second. "Don't go there, fucker. I'm not stupid."

Mike begged to differ. He said nothing. Eventually the guy would give him an out. It was just a matter of time.

"Where is she?" the man shouted louder, shaking his gun erratically. So he wasn't professional. Not by a long shot.

Mike glanced toward the back. "Ran out the door a long time ago. Long gone. Nice try though." He knew he was being antagonistic. He didn't care. The more flustered this asshole got, the easier it would be to take him out.

"You think I'm stupid?"

Well, yes.

"She's in this damn house. Where is she hiding?"

Mike took in the hired man's body language as he shuffled uncomfortably. After all, the guy had lost two other men outside. Were they friends?

Mike nodded toward the hall. "Bathroom. She had to pee?"

The man narrowed his gaze. "Get on the floor. Drop your gun. Hands where I can see them." He wasn't going to shoot Mike. At least he somehow recognized he needed Mike's help to get to Zola.

Mike lowered his gun slowly as the masked man glanced around. His hand shook violently. Any second now, Mike would take a shot. No way was he going to set his gun down. Fat chance. "She's not here, man. You can see that."

The man took a quick step closer to Mike, his hand jerking so the gun waved in Mike's face. "Shut the fuck up. I'm not an idiot. Now tell me where she is."

Mike didn't have a good shot. He couldn't risk lifting his arm to take the guy out with him waving his gun around so erratically.

Suddenly, a shot rang out from Mike's left, and the man in front of him faltered, swaying to the side.

That was all it took for Mike to lift his gun and fire a second shot. Right to the man's forehead. He went down hard.

Mike jerked his gaze toward the kitchen, expecting to find a police officer or a member of SWAT. Instead, he found Zola on her knees, holding a gun, her hands shaking. She hadn't lowered it yet.

Mike scrambled forward, coming up to her side and then slowly removing the gun from her hand—an amazingly nice Sig Sauer. "You were supposed to stay in the safe room."

She jerked her gaze to his, frowning. "You were about to get killed."

"No one was going to kill me."

She lifted one brow. "Really? From where I was sitting, you were defenseless and he had his gun aimed at you." She jerked her gaze to the dead man. "I shot him," she said somberly. It seemed she just now figured that out.

Mike knew how hard it had been for her. She'd never shot a gun in her life, and she'd found herself forced to shoot a human.

"If it makes you feel any better, your shot wasn't fatal. I finished him off."

She nodded, but her gaze was still on the dead guy.

"Where did you get the gun?" He lifted it to see that it was not the average civilian piece.

"From the safe room." She lifted her gaze. "I'm going to have nightmares."

She was also going to get a lecture later about coming out of the safe room, but for the moment, Mike simply wrapped her in one arm and kissed the top of her head as sirens approached.

She swatted at him. "Don't you ever do that to me

again."

He fought the smile tugging at the corners of his mouth while he pulled her face into his neck. "Can't promise that. Unless you find a way to cut down on the number of enemies you have."

She batted at him again with both hands. "You scared me to death. I didn't know if you were dead or alive out here."

"I'm a pretty good shot. Told you that. Those guys didn't stand a chance." He tucked her face toward his chest, pulled them to standing, and led her to the front porch.

"Tex's house," she whispered.

"Yeah. Hope he has good insurance."

She swatted him again.

IT WAS LATE when Mike finally lowered himself to sit on the edge of the bed where Zola was already sprawled out. Another hotel room. Another city. At this rate they would wake up confused every day of their lives. He'd left the light on in the bathroom with the door ajar just to keep them from fumbling around in the night.

"You okay?" she asked, pushing to sitting and leaning over him. She set her chin on his shoulder. Her hair was still damp from a shower, the curls falling in gorgeous ringlets around her face and down his arm.

Ten thousand things raced through his mind, but he needed to get one thing off his chest before it consumed him. "You scared the hell out of me today."

"How?" She lifted her chin.

"I told you to stay in the safe room. You could have been killed."

She groaned. "Seriously, Mike? That's so over-the-top macho of you. A terrorist was holding a gun to your head. Was I supposed to watch you get shot?"

He spun to face her, grabbing her biceps, frowning. "You wouldn't have even known he was there if you had stayed in the safe room."

Her voice rose. "Are you listening to yourself? You were almost killed."

"Are *you* listening to *me*, Zola? *You* could have been killed."

"Well, you would never have known about it from your own grave, Mike." She shrugged out of his grasp and scooted back. Her face was red with anger.

He rubbed his forehead. "You didn't even know how to shoot that gun."

"And yet I managed to do it. There were so many shots. All I could do was imagine you outnumbered and dying. I found that gun in Tex's safe room and knew I had to help if I could."

Why couldn't she see reason?

"Stop looking at me like that. I'm not a damn child, Mike. I'm a woman. A grown woman who is in love with the boyfriend she lost twelve years ago and was not about to risk losing him again. If you can't understand that, then I don't know what else to say." She lowered her face as her words fell.

She loved him. So much she risked her own life for his.

He reached for her chin and lifted her face. "I love you

so much it hurts."

"I know," she whispered.

"I was scared. I'm *still* scared."

"I know."

How could he continue to be mad at her? It was over. He needed to move forward. Continuing to berate her for risking her own safety was pointless. The better plan would be to empower her so that if she ever found herself in a situation like that again, at least she would be able to fire a weapon with enough accuracy to shoot to kill. If he hadn't been there ready to fire the killing blow, the assailant could have turned around and killed her.

He swallowed. "I'm taking you to the firing range first chance we get."

"'Kay," she whispered.

At least she didn't argue that point. He hugged her tighter against his body. "I'm exhausted." He wanted the entire day to disappear. He wanted to bury his face in her hair, inhale her clean scent, and nibble on her ear. But he wasn't kidding. He was beyond tired. Although, he wasn't sure he would be able to fall asleep anytime soon.

The day had been long. It took a while to piece together that the three thugs who tried to capture or kill Zola this second time were hired hitmen. The Johanssons were wealthy, but they struck out a second time. They were also picked up later in the day and wouldn't be given a second opportunity to post bond.

"Sleep." She patted his chest as he lowered onto his back, hugging her against his side. "We're safe."

Were they though? Would Zola ever really be safe while

she spent her days prosecuting terrorists?

He closed his eyes, but his mind raced through the events of the day. He felt horrible about Tex's home, but his friend had assured him repeatedly that the house was insured and Mike wasn't to blame for anything that happened.

Although it would seem unimaginable that anything could have complicated his life any more after the morning they had, he'd been proven wrong.

His boss with the FBI called. He needed him on another assignment. Even though Mike had been scheduled for another week of vacation and he had yet to take more than a few days of said vacation, the government needed him now.

He knew Zola thought he was preoccupied with her safety, and she wasn't wrong, but he was even more concerned with telling her his plans and discussing a future that looked so complicated he couldn't bring himself to face it.

On the one hand, he loved his job and he was good at it. He couldn't imagine giving up his work with the Bureau to move to New Haven. What would he do there?

On the other hand, the mere thought of spending even one night away from Zola at this point brought bile to his throat. He'd lost her for twelve years due mainly to his own stupidity. He didn't intend to lose her again. Not even for twelve hours. But she had a job she loved too. In Connecticut.

"Mike?" Her small hand wandered up and down his chest. "You're so tense. And I know you aren't sleeping."

He sighed, reaching to clasp her hand in his and squeeze it. "Sorry."

She lifted her face and met his gaze again in the dim light of the room. "Don't be sorry. You want to talk? Clear your mind?"

He cringed. "Not really. What I want is for life to be less complicated so I can spend the next seventy years with my woman."

She sighed. "You're worried about what we're going to do next? I mean, with me going back to work and you being assigned God only knows where. Right?"

He stroked a hand through her damp curls. "Seems that's going to happen sooner rather than later."

"What do you mean?" She flattened her palm on his chest.

"My boss called. I didn't want to tell you yet."

She pushed off him so that more space separated them. "Why keep that from me?"

"Because it's a hot mess, and I don't have answers, and it seemed easier to ignore it and enjoy you for another day."

"A day? When do you have to leave? Where are you going?"

"Atlanta. They need me to be there yesterday. I told them Monday."

She nodded, her mouth hanging open. "I see."

He pushed to sitting and hauled her stunned limp body onto his lap. "I'm sorry. I should've told you. I guess I thought if I didn't say it out loud, it wouldn't be true yet."

"But it's real. And we need to discuss it together." She faced him, grabbing his shoulders.

He swallowed. "How the hell are we going to work this out? You have a job you love in Connecticut. I have a job I love that's sending me to Atlanta. A townhome in North Carolina is a long daily commute."

She smiled, though he thought it was forced. "I'm not sure a daily commute is reasonable."

"And I'm not interested in sleeping in two different cities." He leaned back against the headboard, still holding her, tipping his head to face the dark ceiling. "I need to resign."

"You can't resign. You'd resent me for the rest of our lives. I know you. You need to keep this job. *I'll* resign."

He lowered his face to shoot her a narrowed look. "And that's just as absurd. You worked your whole life for this position with the DA. In fact, that's the precise reason your dad didn't want us to get together in the first place twelve years ago. He'd have a coronary if you did that. And so would I."

"Which is precisely why you took his advice and left me alone."

"Well, yes."

"You planning to break up with me again now?" She pushed his arms away from her, climbed off him, and scooted to stand next to the bed. "Mike? Is that what you're holding back? You think we should end this thing because it seems insurmountable and neither of us wants to give up our jobs?"

He stiffened, following her to the edge of the bed and then remaining seated when she backed up with her hands out. "No." He shook his head. "Not a chance in hell. We are *not* going to break up. *Ever.* Got me?" He watched her bite her bottom lip, tears welling up in the corners of her eyes. "Baby, you mean more to me than any stupid job. The only reason I didn't tell you about the Atlanta gig yet was because I was trying to come up with a solution."

She nodded. Too hard. A tear slid down her face. "Let me quit. Please, Mike. It's not that one of us has to be a martyr. Don't look at it that way. Think of it as us making the most economical choice. My job pays shit. It's practically below the poverty level. So let's keep yours. I'll find work in Georgia. I don't have to work in New Haven. They hire lawyers all over the country."

He stared at her for a while, watching her body language as she folded her arms and cocked a hip. She hated the idea of leaving New Haven. No matter what her words were, they didn't match her stance. He groaned and rubbed his forehead with two fingers. "That's not a good option."

"You have a better one?"

"Yeah, I already said it. I'll move to New Haven. I can also easily get a job. I can do lots of things."

"They have a big call for FBI agents who specialize in biological warfare in Connecticut all the sudden?"

"No. But I'm a biologist first. And an agent second. I don't have to continue to work for the FBI." Could he do it? Could he quit and walk away?

Fuck yes. And he would.

"That idea sucks, Mike. You can't do it." She shook her head again.

"Another reason to stay in Connecticut is because your dad is there. You're the only one of us who even has family, and I know you've always been close to him. I don't want to move you away from your father."

"Right now I'm kinda pissed at him, and you should be too."

He shrugged. "We'll both get over it. He's your father. He's only ever had your best interests at heart. Maybe he made some poor choices, but he meant well."

"He meant well?" Her voice rose as she unfolded her crossed arms and held them out. "He ruined twelve years of my life with his antics, Mike."

"I know, baby." Mike spoke calmly, hoping to convince her to forgive the man. It wasn't that Mike wasn't also seething inside over lost time, but he wanted her to reconcile with her dad and move on at the same time. His spine wasn't so flexible that he would permit the man to continue to manipulate the two of them, but the past was the past. It was time to forgive. And it seemed in the few conversations he'd had with Richard that the man genuinely wished them well.

A tear finally slid down her face. She wiped it away. "Maybe I need some time away from Connecticut to cool off anyway."

"Come here." He held out a hand.

She wiped away another tear and padded toward him until he could reach out and grab her around the waist, nestling her body between his knees.

He wiped the next tear away with the pad of his thumb. "Forgive him. It will eat at you until you do. And moving to another state won't make things better."

"How can you be so forgiving?"

"I told you. Because I know what it's like to not have any family. I'd give anything to see either of my parents, and I'd take them any way I could. Drug addicts, criminals, I don't care. It would be worth it to have one hour with them. I won't let you squander that ability."

She didn't say anything, but she watched his face.

Suddenly, he was certain he would quit. He had no idea why he'd been hesitant. It was a job. He could get one anywhere. She meant so much more to him than his position with the FBI. "It's just a job, baby. I would be miserable in Atlanta without you. And I would fret about you leaving your position all the time. It's final. I'll call my boss first thing in the morning and resign. We'll go back to Connecticut and I'll move into your condo."

A sob escaped her lips. "You're sure? It's not even that big."

He rolled his eyes. "You have a bed?"

"Of course."

"Is it a twin?"

"No. You've seen my place."

He gave her a wry smile. "That's all I need." He shook his head. "That's not true. I would even sleep with you on a twin mattress. Or hell, the floor. I don't care where. I just need to be with you." He hugged her body against his tighter and leaned forward to set his lips on her ear. "Discussion over."

She shuddered.

"I love you, Zola."

"I love you too, Mike."

"Settled. We'll get married, move into your place, and

start working on those kids. You still want 2.6 kids, right?" he teased. "That's what you always told me when we were young."

She sniffled. "Stop making me cry."

He closed the distance and set his lips on hers, whispering against her mouth. "Maybe we could do something to lighten the mood."

"I thought you were tired," she mumbled back.

"Changed my mind. I can sleep next week while you work and I'm jobless. Perhaps I could become a kept man." He lifted his brows. "I like that plan. I'll lounge around all day while you work. Maybe pick up a soap opera or two."

She smiled. "You wouldn't last two hours."

"Try me."

GREG LAMBERT LEANED back in the comfortable leather armchair, threading his fingers behind his head. He met the gaze of Vice President Warren Angelo and sighed. "You realize the stakes are higher than you thought, right?"

"Yes. I'm clear on that." Angelo nodded, taking a sip of his bourbon.

Benedict Hughes cleared his throat. "We're fighting this war on several fronts now. The CIA is aware of the new development."

Greg shot his gaze toward Hughes. "It's hardly a new concept. Our own citizens have turned against us before. I'm just pointing out that everyone you hire needs to be diligent and aware that they aren't always looking for a Middle Eastern profile. Terrorists come in all flavors. No one has a monopoly on hatred."

"You think these thugs the Johanssons hired were working for a terrorist organization?" Angelo asked.

Greg shook his head. "I don't think it matters. The point is, they took this job just as easily as anyone else could have. And terrorists can easily prey on locals to do their dirty work for them. People join extremist movements all the time for a variety of reasons, including our own citizens. Half the time I'm not even convinced they realize what they're fighting against or for. They're just messed up individuals who feel the world owes them for some conceived wrong."

Hughes sighed. "Point taken. You got your next SEAL lined up?"

"Yes. I'll be in contact with him tomorrow."

"We appreciate your service, Lambert." The vice president was stoic as he spoke, his brow furrowed. "Without you, countless lives would've been lost in recent months."

"It's my pleasure to serve my country." Greg stood, set his glass on the end table, and headed for the door.

There was no doubt the job was thankless, but he wouldn't want to be in any other position at the moment. Serving his country. Saving lives.

Epilogue

One year later…

Z OLA WAS EXHAUSTED. Mentally and physically. She sat on the floor in the second bedroom they'd converted into a nursery and rocked back and forth, holding the colicky baby girl. She was afraid to sit on the rocking chair for fear she would fall asleep and drop Liza.

Tears ran down her face in the dark. It was the middle of the night. She had to go back to work tomorrow. Her six weeks were up.

She closed her eyes and fought back a sob, biting her lip.

Liza continued to squirm, fighting sleep. She had just nursed. She had a dry diaper. Her life was perfect, but still she wouldn't sleep. The only way to get her to stop crying was to hold her.

"Please, baby girl," Zola pleaded softly, hugging the bundle to her chest.

A shadow fell over the two of them, and Zola lifted her face to find Mike leaning in the doorway. "You okay, babe?"

She nodded, unable to speak for fear she would reveal the barely held-back tears.

He was too sharp though. He eased into the room, crouched in front of her, and looked from her to their daughter. "I think she's asleep, babe." He gently lifted her from Zola's arms and set her in her crib. "Come on," he whispered.

He took her hand and urged her to stand, leading her from the room.

Zola's tears fell without her permission.

Mike led her to their room, sat on the edge of their bed, and dragged her between his legs to hold her. He brushed a long lock of hair from her cheek. "Talk to me."

She shook her head, knowing if she did, she would break down into an ugly cry. Instead, she set her head on his chest and held his biceps. She continued rocking into him as though she were still holding the baby.

He rubbed her arms, always comforting her. He'd been the best damn husband she could ask for. They hadn't even been married yet when she realized she'd missed several pills during their run from the damn terrorists.

Nevertheless, he'd done nothing but hold her hair and rub her back during the early weeks when she'd been too shocked at the idea of being pregnant to even accept it. And then he'd been to every single appointment and asked all the right questions and read the baby books and put together the crib when she was still in denial and let her squeeze his hand to death at the birth and changed diapers… The list went on.

And he was still with her. Holding her. Rubbing her back. Soothing her with his words.

She knew what he thought. She knew he assumed she was suffering from some level of postpartum depression. And maybe she was, but that wasn't the real problem. And she had to tell him. It was the eleventh hour of the eleventh month.

"Zola." His voice was firmer. "Talk to me, babe."

She swallowed back her tears. She had to tell him. She lifted her face and shoved off him, putting a few inches between them. "I can't do it."

He nodded slowly. "Okay. Okay. It's gonna be okay, babe. You can't do what exactly?" He reached for her biceps to tug her closer. "I mean, don't get me wrong. I'm totally here for you. Whatever you need. I can quit my job if you need. We can make it work. If you want me to stay home instead of putting Liza in daycare, give you a break, take on more of the household chores. I can do this."

She stared at him. He was so far off base. And he was so damn fucking awesome. He would hand her the moon. She knew that. Why was it so hard to admit this weird convoluted piece of defeat as if she were less of a person?

He furrowed his brow. "Zola? Tell me." He looked genuinely scared. "Is it me?" He swallowed. "Am I smothering you? Not picking up enough slack? We can get a counselor. Whatever you think." His grip made her close her eyes.

She took a deep breath and shook her head. "No. Mike. It's not you." She exhaled forever and forced herself to continue. "I didn't know it would feel like this. I would never have believed it. I thought people were crazy."

"The depression? Hon, it's perfectly normal. It happens to thousands of women every year. They have meds for that. We'll get through it."

She shook her head more vehemently. And then she shook her husband more vehemently. "Mike, shut up. Listen to me."

"Sorry." He pursed his lips. His eyes were wide with fear.

"I can't leave her."

"What?" He jerked in shock.

"I know. I know." She lowered her gaze. "I'm supposed to be this high-power attorney and all. I've worked my ass off for this career. I made you quit your job to move here and be miserable. You work at a shit company doing something you hate, and you do it for me. I've made a total mess of things. But I didn't know it would feel like this."

She lifted her face. "I didn't know I would love her so much. I didn't know it would tear my heart out to leave her for even an hour. I can't go to work tomorrow. I can't go to work for eighteen years."

Mike looked startled for a moment. His eyes slowly widened again as she watched his expression. And then a smile spread across his face, and he laughed. He tipped his head back and laughed so hard she got annoyed.

"This is serious, Mike. Why the hell are you laughing?"

He tugged her closer and kissed her forehead. "Zola. Baby. It's okay. You scared the hell out of me. I thought you were going off the deep end with depression. And all this time you've been struggling over the decision to go back to work?"

"Basically, yes." It made her sick every time she thought about it. She didn't care about the sleepless nights or the feedings or the crying or the exhaustion. She didn't want to miss a moment of Liza's life. Not a single second.

He laughed again.

"You're not disappointed in me? Or mad? If I quit my job, we'll struggle to pay the rent."

He kissed her lips gently. "Not worried at all. If you want to switch, we'll switch. I can get a better job in a heartbeat."

She batted her eyes, feeling her face grow heated and pink. "Actually…"

"What?" He sounded nervous.

"Your boss has called me several times since Liza was born. He called me several times before she was born too."

"My boss?"

She shook her head. "Not your current boss. Your boss at the FBI."

"He called you? Why?" He narrowed his gaze.

"To see how I was doing. Or perhaps to feel me out to see if he could get you back."

"Seriously?"

"Yes. Apparently the guy they hired in Atlanta left. They still need someone. I think your boss was hoping I would fall into the mom trap and give up my job."

"I can't believe it. He spoke to you about me?"

"Well, he didn't come right out and directly say any of that, but I read between the lines. He was feeling me out."

Mike smirked. "Then it's already decided."

"Well, I don't mean to make you feel trapped. We can discuss it. We can—"

He cut her off. "Stop trying to be all diplomatic, baby. It's a perfect plan." He squeezed her arms again, and then his face fell. "Wait. You're willing to move to Atlanta?"

She chewed on her lower lip. That was the hardest part. But yes. She was. "Yes. It's perfect really. You'll get to do what you love. I'll get to stay home with the baby—my new love—and my dad can visit every few weeks or I'll come up here. We can make it work."

"And you'll be okay not working? It's been your life dream."

She shrugged. "I did it. I'm moving on. It seemed like the most important thing in the world to me. But then Liza came. And now she is. Does that make sense?"

He smiled at her. "Perfect. I love you so much."

"I love you too. I'm sorry I couldn't bring myself to tell you. I felt like a failure somehow. Millions of women work and raise kids. I'm defective or something."

He chuckled. "You're not defective. Everybody's different. No one will fault you for raising our daughter." He kissed her lips this time, nibbling a path to her ear. When he whispered against the sensitive globe, she shuddered. "I'm so relieved. I thought you were pulling away from me."

"Never."

"I love you. I love Liza too."

"I know," she told his shoulder. "I love you too."

He pulled back. "Then it's settled. We're moving to Atlanta."

"Yep."

He leaned his forehead against hers. "Now, I figure we have about fifteen minutes before that hellion starts screaming again. Mind if we spend it making out?"

"Actually, I'm officially back in business. I'd rather we spent it making love."

He groaned. "Even better. Even better, baby."

Thank you to everyone for picking up this fourth book in the **Sleeper SEALs** series. This multi-author branded series includes twelve standalone books by some of your favorite romantic suspense authors. These stories can be read in any order. You can check out the rest of the books in the series on our website: www.SleeperSEALs.com/series-books.

Susan Stoker – PROTECTING DAKOTA – 9/5/17
Becky McGraw – SLOW RIDE – 9/26/17
Dale Mayer – MICHAELS' MERCY – 10/3/17
Becca Jameson – SAVING ZOLA – 10/17/17
Sharon Hamilton – BACHELOR SEAL – 10/31/17
Elle James – MONTANA RESCUE – 11/14/17
Maryann Jordan – THIN ICE – 11/28/17
Donna Michaels – GRINCH REAPER – 12/12/17
Lori Ryan – ALL IN – 1/9/18
Geri Foster – BROKEN SEAL – 1/23/18
Elaine Levine – FREEDOM CODE – 2/6/18
J.M. Madden – FLAT LINE – 2/20/18

AUTHOR'S NOTE

Thanks for taking the time to explore my first military-themed story. I hope you enjoyed this fourth book in the Sleeper SEALs series.

If you're curious about Mike Dorsen's life before this series, check out The Underground series. This gritty series follows the lives of six Russian mixed martial arts fighters and the women they fall in love with. It doesn't have to be read in order, but there is an underlying crime that spans all six books of the series, making it will be more enjoyable if you start from the beginning.

Force (The Underground, Book 1)

Here's a blurb for Force:

Lauren Schneider has been hiding from the Russians for six months. She's stir crazy and finds it difficult to believe anyone is still hunting her. After all, the leader of the mob, Anton Yenin, who had her kidnapped in the first place, is behind bars. Why would he continue to pine over her? And then there's Dmitry. That man is smoking hot...with his shaved head, tattooed arms, and bulging muscles. If he doesn't make a move for her soon, she will self-combust.

Dmitry Volikov is a member of Anton Yenin's stable of fighters. However, he secretly rescued Lauren from the Russians and has done everything in his power to keep her sequestered and therefore safe. His motives aren't purely altruistic. He's been in love with the gorgeous Lauren for over half a year. He and his partner, Mikhail, work hard at construction sites during the day, still managing to work out in the early mornings and fight for the underground MMA circuit on Friday nights. They're supporting not only Lauren, but Mikhail's sister, Alena.

Lauren is done hiding. When she sneaks out and gets a job at a local bar, Dmitry becomes frantic worrying about her safety—and by default his. If anyone finds her, she's dead. If anyone finds her with him, they're both dead. But Lauren is hard-headed. There's no stopping her. Even their bourgeoning steamy relationship isn't enough to keep her from defying logic. In the bedroom, she enjoys Dmitry's dominant ways, but when it comes to the rest of her life, she's hell on wheels.

Yenin won't be in jail much longer, so time is running out. When he's released, there's little doubt he'll round up his fighters. Paranoia sets in for both Dmitry and Lauren. Anyone could be following them. Or maybe they're being ridiculously cautious. In any case, Dmitry is facing the fight of his life. He can't leave Lauren at home, and she's a moving target in the crowded underground venue. He has no choice but to rely on his close friends to keep her safe during the fight, but when all hell breaks loose, will it destroy their world?

If you're interesting in trying out one of my paranormal stories, I have recently released a new series called Arcadian Bears. This series is a spin-off from my most popular series, Wolf Masters. The first book, *Grizzly Mountain*, released April 11, 2017. Here's a blurb:

Two grizzly shifters rarely bind themselves together in

haste, but when one partner knows nothing of their species, complications mount.

Heather Simmons is excited to start a new job in Alberta, Canada, as a glaciologist. But when a minor accident leaves her trapped on a hiking trail overnight, she finds herself facing a burly mountain man and a pair of grizzly bears. From that moment forward, things could not get weirder.

Isaiah Arthur knows instinctively that Heather is his mate the moment he scents her clothing before heading up the mountain to rescue her. The sensation is confusing since she is obviously human, and converting a human to his species is strictly forbidden.

A rogue shifter takes Heather's transition out of Isaiah's hands, however. Isaiah is left with no choice but to take her home and find a way to inform her of her unintended fate, while fighting the intense need to make her his as soon as possible.

The North American governing body, the Arcadian Council, is not amused by the rare turning of a human, and chaos ensues as Isaiah races against the clock to bind his mate to him forever before someone steps in the way and takes the opportunity out of his hands.

Go here to read an excerpt or find purchasing links!
beccajameson.com/arcadian-bears/grizzly-mountain

BOOKS BY BECCA JAMESON

Wolf Masters Series
Kara's Wolves
Lindsey's Wolves
Jessica's Wolves
Alyssa's Wolves
Tessa's Wolf
Rebecca's Wolves
Melinda's Wolves
Laurie's Wolves
Amanda's Wolves
Sharon's Wolves

Arcadian Bears Series
Grizzly Mountain
Grizzly Beginning
Grizzly Secret
Grizzly Promise

The Fight Club Series
Come
Perv
Need
Hers
Want
Lust

The Underground Series
Force
Clinch
Guard
Submit
Thrust
Torque
Saving Sofia

Sleeper SEALs Series
Saving Zola

Spring Training Series
Catching Zia
Catching Lily
Catching Ava

Claiming Her Series
The Rules
The Game
The Prize

Emergence Series
Bound to be Taken
Bound to be Tamed
Bound to be Tested
Bound to be Tempted

Durham Wolves Series
Rescue in the Smokies
Fire in the Smokies
Freedom in the Smokies

Wolf Gatherings Series
Tarnished
Dominated
Completed
Redeemed
Abandoned
Betrayed

Stand Alone Books
Blind with Love
Guarding the Truth
Out of the Smoke
Abducting His Mate
Three's a Cruise
Wolf Trinity
Frostbitten

ABOUT THE AUTHOR

Becca Jameson is the best-selling author of the Wolf Masters series and The Fight Club series. She lives in Atlanta, Georgia, with her husband and two kids. With over 60 books written, she has dabbled in a variety of genres, ranging from paranormal to sports to military to BDSM. When she isn't writing, she can be found jogging with her dog, scrapbooking, or cooking. She doesn't sleep much, and she loves to talk to fans, so feel free to contact her through e-mail, Facebook, or her website.

…where Alphas dominate…

Email:
Beccajameson4@aol.com

Facebook:
facebook.com/becca.jameson.18

website:
beccajameson.com

twitter:
twitter.com/beccajameson

Newsletter:
beccajameson.com/newsletter-sign-up

64133714R00155

Made in the USA
Middletown, DE
09 February 2018